D1115993

S.C.

A.M.

BY EMMA HARRISON

smart novels
SAT VOCABULARY

© 2006, 2008 by Spark Publishing

All rights reserved. No part of this publication may be reproduced, stored in a retrieval system, or transmitted, in any form or by any means, electronic, mechanical, photocopying, recording, or otherwise, without prior written permission from the publisher.

SPARKNOTES is a registered trademark of SparkNotes LLC.

Spark Publishing
A Division of Barnes & Noble
120 Fifth Avenue
New York, NY 10011
www.sparknotes.com

ISBN-13: 978-1-4114-0441-0
ISBN-10: 1-4114-0441-6

Library of Congress Cataloging-in-Publication Data

Harrison, Emma.
  S.C.A.M.: an SAT vocabulary novel / by Emma Harrison.
    p. cm.—(SAT vocabulary novel)
  Summary: After catching his girlfriend cheating on him on what should be the best day of his life, Mike Riley, a star high school quarterback well on his way to an athletic scholarship at the school of his choice, it takes a night of poker to make him feel like a winner again.

  ISBN-13: 978-1-4114-0441-0
  ISBN-10: 1-4114-0441-6
  [1. Poker—Fiction. 2. Football—Fiction. 3. Dating (Social customs)—Fiction. 4. High schools—Fiction. 5. Schools—Fiction.] I. Title. II. Title: SCAM : an SAT vocabulary novel. III. Series: SAT vocabulary novels.

PZ7.H2485Sca 2006
[Fic]—dc22

                                                              2006008869

Please submit changes or report errors to www.sparknotes.com/errors.

Printed and bound in the United States

10 9 8 7 6 5

SAT is a registered trademark of the College Entrance Examination Board, which was not involved in the production of, and does not endorse, this book.

ACT is a registered trademark of ACT, Inc., which was not involved in the production of, and does not endorse, this book.

"I'll tell you what your problem is, Mike. You *suck* at bluffing," Tyler Brooks said, tossing a couple more chips into the pot in the center of the table. "You just don't have a **mendacious** nature. And that is why . . . I am going . . . to kick . . . your . . . *ass.*"

The other guys around the felt-topped poker table laughed. I **feigned** concern as Tyler turned his baseball cap around backward and leaned back in his chair. I let him smile his triumphant smile for a moment, delaying his misery for fun. Hey. At least I admit it. I enjoy taking my friends down. That's what poker's all about, isn't it?

Well, unless you're in it for the money. But considering our biggest pot to date was a whopping forty-two bucks, no one around here was going home a zillionaire. Nope. Our games were really just excuses to get together and talk smack.

"And *your* problem is, Brooksy, you're a **bombastic** ass," I replied, calling his bet. "Let's see what you got."

"Full house. Ladies over tens," Tyler announced, turning his two hole cards over. Sure enough—when added to the communal cards, he did have a fairly sweet hand. Three queens and two tens. Not bad at all. But not as good as . . .

"**Foiled** again, my friend," I said, turning over my two threes.

"Oh!" the guys around the table cheered and groaned.

Tyler's face fell with a satisfying plop. Ian O'Connor, my best friend and the ultimate poker host, reached over to slap my hand. Add my threes to the two in the river and that gave me four of a kind. It had been **audacious** of me, calling Tyler's bet with two tens out there as well. He could have had four tens, after all. But I took my chances. It's not often that I do that. My betting style is usually

---

mendacious: dishonest **bombastic:** overblown **audacious:** bold
feigned: faked **foiled:** thwarted

based on my **innate parsimony**. But sometimes, you just gotta roll the dice.

"He totally *waxed* your ass!" Brad Lackler cried mirthfully.

"Shut up, Lackler," Tyler grumbled.

"It *is* a shame how four little threes can beat your big old royals," I said.

"Dude, you suck," Tyler whined, throwing his cards down.

"Beg to differ," I shot back, reaching out to gather my winnings. "These chips beg to differ too, by the way."

Ian reached over his head and stretched, glancing at the pool-ball wall clock on the far side of his **spacious** basement. Every Friday night the guys met up here for a few games, a couple of sodas (or beers when we could come by them), and some laughs. You'd think Ian's parents would break up the party once in a while, but being one of the richest kids in Hillside was not without its **perks**. Ian's folks were out half the time at some **charitable** function or another, and when they *were* home, their house was so damn big they never even realized we were down here.

"It's about that time, fellas," Ian said, gathering up the cards. He glanced in my direction. We all knew I had to get home before football curfew. On the nights before games we all had to be home by ten o'clock. Every once in a while Coach even went down the **roster** and cold-called our houses to make sure we were there. Some guys managed to get their parents to lie for them, but Coach had figured out the ploy and always insisted on speaking directly to his players.

"No way!" Tyler complained. "One more game. You gotta give me a chance to win my money back."

Ian glanced at me and I shrugged. "Fine by me," I said. I had some time. And we all knew Tyler wouldn't be **mollified** until I gave in. He was the sorest loser of the group.

"All right. One more," Ian said.

---

innate: inherent	**perks:** benefits	**roster:** list of players
parsimony: stinginess	**charitable:** for charity	**mollified:** calmed
spacious: roomy		

He shuffled and dealt the cards. I pulled my hole cards to me and checked the corners. Total crap. A seven and a three, unsuited. A lesser man would have folded right there, but in my innate **munificence** I tossed a couple chips in the pot anyway. Let Tyler have a chance at a bigger take. What did I care? I was going home twenty bucks up anyway. Besides, I knew if I folded right off the bat, he would have made a scene.

"So, you guys wanna come over my place tomorrow for the Yankee game?" Tyler asked, toying with his chips as Ian dealt the flop. "Dad said he'd swing a couple six packs if you all stay over."

"Cool," Ian said. "I'm in."

"Your dad rocks," Brad added.

Chris Templeman, our fifth, was in as well. I shifted in my seat as everyone looked at me.

"What about you, bluffer?" Tyler asked. "Can't turn down baseball and brew."

"Actually, he already has plans," Ian announced. "With *Marcy.*"

"Aw, yeah," Brad **intoned**. Tyler made a whipping sound, and everyone laughed.

"Blow her off, man," Chris said, placing his bet on the flop. "This is **sanctioned** booze we're talking about here."

"I can't," I said, my face heating up. This was going to hurt. "It's our anniversary."

"Aw!" they all chorused. Kissing noises and a few inappropriate groans followed. "Wittle Mikey's got a wifey," Chris teased. I stared straight at the pot as my face burned.

"Is cheerleader-girl finally gonna give it up?" Tyler asked. "'Cuz if she is then you are *definitely* off the hook. That girl has got a *sick—*"

"Dude. Back off," I said flatly. They could tease me all they wanted, but I wasn't going to let them talk about my girlfriend like that. Even if they were my best friends. Marcy was the coolest. She was smart and athletic and totally unclingy, unlike all my friends'

---

munificence: generosity   **intoned:** spoke musically   **sanctioned:** approved

girlfriends. Lately I'd been thinking that I was probably even in love with her. Not that I would ever admit that to these morons.

"Sorry," Tyler said sarcastically under his breath. As if he didn't get why I was so touchy. "So, you gonna bet or what?"

I didn't even need to look at my cards again. "No. I fold."

"Oh, man!" Tyler cried, **exasperated** with me.

"Dude, get over it." I glanced at my watch. "I gotta go anyway. I gotta be at the field at eight o'clock. Coach gives us extra laps if we're late on game day."

"That's right, man. Big game. Break a leg tomorrow," Brad said, glancing up as I passed him by.

"Yeah, man. Peace," Tyler added, slapping hands with me.

"Dude. Cash me out?" I asked Ian.

He shoved the deck of cards in his back pocket as he stood. The Vegas casinos never would have gone for such a **brazen breach** of **conduct** as the dealer getting up in the middle of a game, but we were a bit more casual around here. He took my chips and counted out my cash, keeping the **requisite** ten percent cut for the house. Like Ian needed any more money. But hey, I didn't **begrudge** him his earnings. The weekly game was his idea, and he did supply all the junk food that we **devoured** every week.

"Kick a little Wildcat ass tomorrow," he said, slapping the cash into my hand.

"You got it, brotha," I replied.

Then I headed out into the night to a chorus of "good luck"s. I had to laugh as I closed the door behind me. My friends were so **predictable**. The only thing that always got me out of a poker game without a huge **clamor** of protest was a previous football commitment. In Hillside it was all about school spirit.

*   *   *   *   *

exasperated: irritated	**conduct:** normal behavior	**devoured:** ate greedily
brazen: defiant	**requisite:** required	**predictable:** unsurprising
breach: violation	**begrudge:** disapprove	**clamor:** noise

"They think they're coming into our house and taking us down?!" Curtis Springer shouted, pacing up and down the locker room in his shoulder pads and football pants. "Naw, man! No way do they come in to *our* house and take us down. You feel me?!"

The team roared its approval, and we all cheered and hollered. Springer's pregame rile-ups were a long-honored tradition. Nothing got the adrenaline pumping better. I yanked my jersey over my head and was about to join in an **impromptu** huddle when Coach Rinaldi called my name from his office.

"Riley! Riley! Hey! Get in here!"

My heart dropped, and I caught Curtis's eye as the crowd around him grew more and more **frenetic**. He shrugged and got back to his ritual. I grabbed my helmet and followed after Coach. I knew I hadn't done anything wrong. Anyone who knows me will tell you I am the **epitome** of the goody-goody—that it's next to impossible for Mike Riley to do anything wrong. But that didn't mean that being called out by authority figures didn't still freak me out.

"What's up, Coach?" I asked, stepping into his small, square office.

"Have a seat," he said, easing onto his rickety chair.

He pulled the red baseball cap from his head and scratched at the bald spot in the center of the ring of blond hair. Uh-oh. This was serious. I sat on the edge of the vinyl seat, my heart pounding. I guess this was another way to kick-start the adrenaline.

"Mike, I called you in here to let you know that there are scouts in the bleachers today," he said. "A couple of the SUNYs are coming out to have a look and **assess** your performance."

I felt like someone had just handed me a ticket to the Super Bowl. "They're here for me?" I asked.

"Of course they are. Who else?" Coach Rinaldi asked. "As far as I recall, you're the only one here who broke two of the longest-standing New York State high school passing records last year."

---

impromptu: spontaneous   **epitome:** ideal example   **assess:** evaluate
frenetic: frenzied

I beamed with pride. Scouts. Here for me. This was it. This was my chance at a scholarship. I had been hoping for a **boon** like this my entire life but had never allowed myself to believe it would actually happen. Ever since I was fourteen years old I had been working odd and part-time jobs, trying to save up for college. My parents are both teachers, and they love their jobs, but we've all known for a long time that we were going to fall into that financial catch-22—that we wouldn't have enough money for college tuition but would appear too "well off" for financial aid.

"Now, it's just the state schools this afternoon, not that that's anything to shake a stick at," Coach said, leaning his beefy arms on his desk. "But you do well out there today, get some buzz going, next week we could be hosting some Division One schools. Like Penn State, perhaps."

My throat went completely dry. Penn State. My dream school. The school that everyone who had ever so much as met me knew that I wanted to attend. Pride and excitement were now crowded out by nerves. This had to be the game of my life.

Coach stood up and offered his hand. "This is it, son. Your big break."

I pushed my chair back, almost knocking it over in my manic state, and shook his hand. "Thanks, Coach," I said.

He grinned as the locker room exploded with **raucous** cheers. "Make me proud."

* * * * *

"Third and twenty? What the hell, you guys?" I seethed in the huddle, hoping my teammates would pick up on my **ardor** and use it. We were on the Wildcats' forty-five, when two minutes ago we had been on their twenty-five. One minute we were driving down the field, the **archetypal** dominant offense, and the next we were the complete

---

boon: blessing   **ardor:** zeal   **archetypal:** exemplary
raucous: noisy

antithesis of that. I couldn't afford to let my team get **apathetic** on me now. This game was too important—to me and to our record. "No more penalties, all right? They're killing us. Any one of you guys jumps early, you're gonna have me to answer to, you got me?"

The offensive line grumbled their assent. I could hear Morris Johnson, my center, heaving for breath across the huddle.

"Good. Now let's take it to these guys. Their pass rush is for crap. We're better than them, right?" I said.

They all cheered their approval.

"Right! Now we're gonna run the twenty-yard hook. Daryl, get open. You guys give me time, and we'll get six outta this, okay?"

"Yeah!" a few of the guys cheered.

"Ready? Break!"

We moved out of the huddle up to the line of scrimmage. The home crowd was louder than it had been all day. We were down by a **deficit** of three points with two minutes to go. This down was everything. I could practically *feel* the scouts breathing down my neck, **scrutinizing** my every move.

"Blue, sixteen! Blue, sixteen!" I shouted, checking the defensive line, trying to **discern** their strategy. They were definitely coming on the blitz. "Hike!"

The ball hit my hands. The two lines slammed into one another. Helmets cracked, groans spilled out from behind mouth guards and clenched teeth. All I could do was hope my line would not **succumb**, or I was toast. I scanned the field over the linebackers' heads. The cornerback was all up in Daryl's face. Something flashed in the corner of my eye. A defender had broken through. I tucked the ball and ran left, just avoiding the tackle. The guy tumbled to the ground, reaching for my feet. He got a hand on my ankle, but I twisted away. I **scurried** all the way to the sideline. Down field, Daryl executed a **deft** spin move, and his defender ate dirt. I pulled back to throw and said a prayer. Another defender was coming right at me full tilt, so I

antithesis: opposite	**scrutinizing:** examining	**scurried:** scampered
apathetic: spiritless	**discern:** detect	**deft:** skillful
deficit: shortage	**succumb:** give in	

let it fly. The moment the ball left my fingers, this monstrous dude slammed into me and drilled me into the ground.

Time stood still. I couldn't breathe. The dude shoved me farther into the earth as he stood up, but his extra punishment didn't matter. The bleachers exploded in a frenzied cheer, **melodious** to my ears. Daryl had caught the ball. *Touchdown!*

Curtis ran over, cheering in **jubilation**, and yanked me to my feet. I sputtered and coughed and drew in a breath. Everyone was slapping me on the back and helmet, shaking me and hugging me. We rushed off the field, and Danny Leonard kicked the extra point. It was good. The whole place was going nuts, and I couldn't stop grinning if I'd tried. I had just completed a 45-plus yard touchdown pass under extreme pressure with the game on the line. I knew the scouts were loving it. I had just **justified** their making this trip to see me play.

As our kicking team took the field to kick off, I turned and found Marcy on the sidelines. There she was in her red and black cheer-leading uniform, her auburn hair pulled back in a ponytail, looking every bit as gorgeous as an MTV backup dancer. She waved and blew me a kiss, and I felt like I was on top of the world. Life just didn't get any better than this.

*   *   *   *   *

I was lighter than air when I came out of the locker room after the game. My wet hair was slicked back from my head, and I wore a clean Hillside Cardinals T-shirt. Everyone was cheering and talking **boisterously**, making plans to hit the diner and hang, holding on to the post-win **euphoria**. All I could think about was finding my parents and Marcy. I definitely wanted to share this feeling with them.

My parents were waiting for me just outside the gym. Dad was wearing his favorite Cardinals Football sweatshirt and jeans, while

melodious: musical	**justified:** warranted	**euphoria:** great happiness
jubilation: joy	**boisterously:** loudly, rowdily	

mom had gone with the more formal fan look—a red turtleneck and chinos. She clutched a plastic mini-pompom in her hand. Her dark hair was curled and perfect, as always, while dad's usually messy hair was hidden under a baseball cap. His theory was that if he had to look put-together all week to be a good role model for his students, he could get a little **slovenly** on the weekends.

"Mike! Great game!" my father said, giving me the handshake/one-shouldered hug.

"Thanks, Dad," I replied with a grin.

"Are you all right?" my mother asked, checking me over. She has a **propensity** for coddling me after games, especially games in which I get crushed by **malevolent** linebackers.

"I'm fine, Mom. I promise," I said, wanting to **palliate** her concern. "That hit wasn't as **heinous** as it looked."

"Well, they should have penalized him, if you ask me," she said with a huff. My father and I laughed.

"Well, you're kind of **biased**, Mom," I said. "It was a clean hit. Trust me."

"If you say so," she said **grudgingly**.

"Lori, please. The boy is fine," my father said. "Better than fine. You know, the scout from Buffalo wants to stop by the house later."

"You're kidding!" I said, **elated**.

"He seemed *very* interested," my mother added with obvious pride.

"I don't believe it," I said. "It's all happening."

"We couldn't be happier for you, kid," my dad said, giving me a real hug this time.

"Thanks, Dad." I pulled back, enjoying the moment. Then I remembered there was someone else I wanted to celebrate with. I checked my watch. "Sorry, guys. I gotta go meet Marcy," I said. "But I'll catch you at home in a little while."

"Definitely," my mother said. "Tell her we said hello."

"Will do!"

---

slovenly: untidy
propensity: tendency
malevolent: vicious

palliate: ease
heinous: horrific
biased: prejudiced

grudgingly: reluctantly
elated: happy

I pushed my way out into the sunshine, expecting to see Marcy waiting in our usual spot, on the bench under one of the huge oaks on the school's front lawn. The only people there were a few JV cheerleaders, flirting with some **neophyte** JV players. I heard a cheer around back of the gym and thought maybe the celebration had **precluded** her meeting me—that she'd gotten caught up in the insanity between the field and the school. I cut across the grass to the asphalt pathway and was just rounding the outside of the gym when a kid on a skateboard zoomed out of nowhere and cut me off.

"Watch it, jerk!" I shouted, my heart in my throat.

He merely whooped and **skirted** me, followed quickly by three other friends. The last one through was a girl with short blonde hair in a black hoodie who shot me a wink and a smile as she raced by. I narrowed my eyes at her familiar face and realized it was Winter Dumas, kid sister of my former teammate Gray Dumas. She and her brother were totally **disparate**. He was the super-jock and most-school-spirited student, with only **meager** academic skills. She was the **erudite** Goth-chick with a **disgruntled** weekly column in the school newspaper. I had seen her around school with her sun-**eschewing**, **pallid** friends, and she was pretty cute—in that psycho, **disenfranchised** way. Her column did always make me laugh, though.

"Sorry!" she shouted with a shrug.

"Yeah. Whatever," I said under my breath.

My heart rate was just returning to normal as I made my way around the gym. I couldn't wait to find Marcy and get a big congratulatory kiss. I wanted to tell her all about the scouts and the guy from Buffalo. But mostly I wanted to talk about tonight, about our anniversary **excursion**. When she heard the romantic evening I had planned, she was going to **rhapsodize** about what an amazing boyfriend she had.

---

neophyte: beginner
precluded: prevented
skirted: went around
disparate: different

meager: weak
erudite: learned
disgruntled: discontented
eschewing: avoiding
pallid: pale

disenfranchised: excluded
excursion: trip
rhapsodize: speak emotionally

I came around the back corner of the gym, and my heart stopped. Suddenly, all my **meticulous** plans came crashing down around me. This was wrong. It couldn't be. It was an **aberration**. But even after I blinked a few times, the scene stayed the same: Pressed up against the brick wall, making out with an **appallingly crude** lack of **modesty**, were a guy in a leather jacket and a girl in a cheerleading uniform. A girl with auburn hair.

My gut twisted in pain and my duffel bag dropped off my shoulder. I'd found Marcy all right, with her tongue down Dominic Thomas's throat.

meticulous: careful
aberration: atypical event
appallingly: shockingly
crude: unrefined
modesty: shyness

Chapter Two

"What the hell is this?" I blurted.

Marcy and Dominic jumped apart. Her face was flushed but went white the moment she saw me. Dominic, however, had to hide his **puerile** smirk by turning away for a moment. Of all the people in all the world she could have chosen to **cuckold** me with, Dominic Thomas was the worst. He was such a slimy tool—with his slick hair, his silver cross around his neck, his leather jacket. And that attitude? Forget it. He'd been **flouting** authority since kindergarten, when he told our gym teacher he wouldn't play basketball with the dorky kids. I mean, who did that? At age five? And he'd only gotten worse with age. I couldn't **fathom** what she was doing with him.

"Mike, I—"

"Marcy, tell me you weren't just kissing this idiot," I said, seething.

"Hey, man. Why don't we all just chill for a sec?" Dominic said, still smirking.

"Get the hell out of here, man," I said **vehemently**. "This is between me and Marcy."

He didn't move. Instead, he looked at her for **corroboration**. The closeness between them was **implicit**, and it almost killed me. Like *he* was going to protect *her* from *me*. She was *my* girlfriend, for God's sake. If anyone was going to do the protecting around here, it was me!

"It's okay," Marcy said **tremulously**.

"You sure?" he asked. He was rubbing it in. He just wanted to **abase** me. I could tell. It was all I could do to keep from punching the **duplicitous** bastard in the face.

---

puerile: childish
cuckold: cheat on
flouting: defying

fathom: understand
vehemently: fiercely
corroboration: confirmation
implicit: implied

tremulously: shakily
abase: undermine
duplicitous: sneaky

"Dude, you better get out of here right now, unless you want the ass-kicking of your life."

Was that **succinct** enough for him? **Apparently** so. He finally raised his hands and **acquiesced**. I waited until he was around the building and out of earshot before I said anything else. I took a deep breath as Marcy eyed me warily.

"What's going on here, Marcy?" I asked calmly, trying to appear **stoic**. I didn't want to come off as a big baby here. I could handle whatever was coming. I hoped. "How long have you been **dissembling**?"

Marcy hesitated a moment, kicking the toe of her cheerleading sneaker into the dirt beneath her feet. "Since the summer," she said finally, hugging herself.

"Two months?!" I blurted, all the blood rushing to my head. So much for being **impervious**. I couldn't believe she had been sneaking around behind my back for two whole months! "How? When? And why him? God, Marcy. I **abhor** Dominic Thomas! You know that! Did you just do this to hurt me?"

"No!" she cried, her eyes filling with tears. "It just kind of . . . happened. You were off checking out schools with your parents, and he came into Dairy Queen, like, every day, and we just started talking . . ."

I pushed my hands into my hair, my mind reeling. Two months. Two months of **guile** and **disingenuous** behavior and of me being totally blind. *Who else knew about this? How big of an idiot am I?*

A tremendous one, I thought. *You had this **elaborate** evening planned for her on the very day you caught her with another guy.*

Our anniversary. She had cheated on me on our anniversary. And for many days before that, apparently.

"I can't believe you did this to me," I said finally, my voice cracking. "I thought . . . I thought . . ."

---

succinct: concise	**dissembling:** being	**disingenuous:** insincere
apparently: seemingly	deceptive	**elaborate:** extravagant
acquiesced: gave in	**impervious:** impenetrable	
stoic: unmoved	**abhor:** hate	
	guile: cunning	

I had thought I was falling in love with her. But I couldn't tell her that now. It seemed so **trite** and **naïve**. And saying it wasn't going to **abate** this pain that was wrenching my heart. It would only make it worse.

Marcy reached out for my arm like she was going to comfort me, but I pulled away. "We're over. Obviously," I said.

A tear spilled down her cheek. "Mike—"

I had to get out of there. If I stood there for one more second I was going to go off on a **tirade** about how she could stuff her **gratuitous** emotion. About how she was the one who had screwed this all up. About how I couldn't believe I had ever trusted someone like her. So instead, I just turned and walked away, ignoring her as she shouted my name.

* * * * *

That evening I sat alone in my living room in front of the Yankees pre-game show, **wallowing** in self-pity. I was so angry that I had actually considered going out and **scouring** the town for a party and some random girl to hook up with, but I had never been a **vindictive** person. That just wasn't me. So instead, I had **resolved** to **repose** on the sofa and think about where it had all gone wrong. I had even drawn all the curtains over the windows to get it as dark in the room as possible. All the better for **vilifying** my ex and **berating** myself for my blindness.

Of course, my glass-is-half-full mother had other ideas.

"Michael, you should really go out to that party Tyler is having," she said, straightening up around me, picking up the empty chip bag and soda cans that were piling up on the coffee table. She had no idea Tyler's dad was offering free beer. If she had, there was no way she would be **prodding** me to go. "Sitting here alone is not going to **allay** the pain of a breakup."

---

trite: unoriginal
naïve: innocent
abate: stop
tirade: rant

gratuitous: unwarranted
wallowing: indulging
scouring: searching
vindictive: spiteful
resolved: decided
repose: lie down

vilifying: slandering
berating: criticizing, chewing out
prodding: urging
allay: ease

She was right, of course. My mother has a certain **acumen** for matters of the heart. But that didn't mean I had to listen to her. For the moment, I needed to feel the **anguish**.

"One night, Mom," I said. "Just let me be depressed, okay?"

"You don't want to talk about it?" she asked hopefully.

I shook my head. For the moment, I was **taciturn**. And besides, if I started talking to her about it, she might get a glimpse of my **severe enmity** toward Marcy, and I didn't want her to see that. I'd talk to her about it when I'd had more time to cool off.

She smiled at me in a **forlorn** way, all my garbage gathered up in her arms. "I'll order you a pizza. Sausage and peppers good?"

I managed to lift the corners of my mouth. "Thanks."

As she left the room, Ian walked in. I guess my father had let him into the house. I was so out of it I hadn't even heard the doorbell.

"Maybe you can cheer him up," my mother told him as they passed each other in the doorway.

"You got it, Mrs. Riley," he said. Then she was gone, and he eyed me **dubiously**. "Dude. You look like death."

"That's what happens when you find out that **fidelity** is too much to ask for from the girl you love," I said **acerbically**.

Ian sighed. He dropped down onto the couch next to me. "I **empathize**, Mike. I do," he said. "You remember how crushed I was when Becky broke up with me."

I nodded and sat up a little. This was exactly what I needed—someone to **validate** the pit of despair I was **mired** in.

"And that's why I'm here to tell you that this should be a day of celebration, my friend!" he cheered.

"What?" I blurted. This had just taken a weird turn.

"It's **imperative**, Mike! The **yoke** is off! You're free! You should be out there partying, having a good time!" he cheered, grasping my shoulder. "Now let's go over to Tyler's house and get ourselves hammered!"

---

acumen: intelligence	**dubiously:** doubtfully	**validate:** confirm
anguish: pain	**fidelity:** faithfulness	**mired:** stuck
taciturn: quiet	**acerbically:** bitterly	**imperative:** necessary
severe: extreme	**empathize:** feel compassion	**yoke:** burden
enmity: hostility	for	
forlorn: sad		

I sighed. "You sound like my mom."

"Your mom told you to get hammered?" he asked.

I smirked. "No. She wants me to go out though. She doesn't want me to **foster** my depression."

"Smart woman," he said. "So let's go. **Sobriety** is not the prescription for a night like this. Believe me."

"Look, man, I appreciate your coming over here. Really," I said. "But I'm not going out. You can if you want, but I just don't feel like it."

"You sure?" he asked.

"I'm sure," I said **decisively**.

"That's cool, brotha," he said, sitting back as the Yankees took the field. "Team's gonna play the same whether I'm here or there."

"Thanks."

"No problem, man," he said. "But I really do think this breakup is a good thing. You got better stuff to spend your time on anyway."

"I do?" I asked.

"Are you kidding?" he asked. "Football, school, improving your poker game . . ."

I whacked him in the arm, and he laughed, which made me crack my first real smile since that morning's win. Okay. So maybe everything *was* going to be all right. Eventually.

*　*　*　*　*

On Sunday morning it took a lot of effort for me to pull myself out of bed, but I couldn't spend the entire day **ruminating** about Marcy and her **wanton** ways. I had a history paper due that week, and I had been **remiss** lately, **procrastinating** on the research. So instead of staying under the covers, I showered and dressed and headed for the Hillside Public Library. Normally I would have just hit the Internet, but Mr. Weeks, my history teacher, was an old-school guy with **antiquated** ideas. He wanted us to glean all our facts from

---

foster: encourage
sobriety: soberness
decisively: with certainty

ruminating: thinking
wanton: immoral
remiss: irresponsible

procrastinating: delaying
antiquated: old

actual books and swore he would be able to tell the difference in our work. I wasn't sure if I believed this, but I wasn't about to put it to the test. My grades were too important.

It was **tedious** work, paging through the indexes of all those heavy history **tomes**, but the library's **pacific** atmosphere had a calming effect on me. I sat back in one of the cushioned chairs near the window and **perused** a book on World War I. Around me people whispered, and pages turned, and suddenly I realized my negative feelings were starting to **wane**. Yesterday had been awful, obviously, but here I was, doing my homework, having another day. The world had not come to a **catastrophic** end.

I found the section I was looking for, on Germany's role in the war, and took out my notebook. As I was scratching various notes and ideas out on the page, I saw something out of the corner of my eye. I looked up just as someone outside the window went careening by on a skateboard, jumped the parking lot's curb, and landed on the asphalt of the **adjacent** playground.

It was Winter Dumas. And she was amazingly **facile** at boarding. She popped up on the small ramp at the far end of the playground and executed a couple of **adroit** turns, grabbing her board and hamming it up. Watching her playing out there in the sun, I was transfixed. Clearly she was having a great time. She even laughed out loud as she spun around and around in the center of the asphalt. Then she raced to the end of the park on her board and took off at a fast clip. I realized the **extreme** maneuver she was about to attempt and my heart stopped. What was she thinking? She was going to crack open her skull!

Winter did an ollie and her board caught air. I held my breath. This was going to be a **debacle**. Her trucks hit the old balance beam, and she slid down the length of it, keeping perfect balance and landing gracefully at the far end. Then she took off to do it all over again.

---

tedious: tiresome
tomes: books
pacific: peaceful
perused: examined

wane: fade
catastrophic: disastrous
adjacent: nearby
facile: effortless

adroit: skilled
extreme: severe
debacle: catastrophe

My heart pounded insanely in my chest. This girl was good. And daring. And **impetuous**. And man, was it sexy.

Winter made another run and another perfect trick. Intrigued, I marked my place in my book and walked outside to the park. I had no idea what to say to her, so I just hovered near the open gate. She saw me and threw a **winsome** smile over her shoulder.

"Hey there, football star," she said, sliding over on her board.

"You know who I am?" I asked.

"Everyone knows who you are," she said. "Besides, you used to hang out at my house with my brother. Don't act like you don't remember. You were always finishing off our Cheetos. I hated that."

I laughed.

"So, what's up?" she asked.

"Not much. Nice skills," I said, pushing my hands into my pockets. Her short hair was pulled back in two tiny ponytails, **accentuating** her rosy skin and bright green eyes. Bright green eyes that glinted mischievously.

"I know," she said with a shrug. "Hey, what're you doing here? Shouldn't you still be off riding on your team's shoulders in victory?" She skated away a bit and worked some turns in the center of the playground.

I smirked. "I guess you think football and school spirit are **vapid**, huh?" I asked.

She shot me a look, like "duh."

"Then what were you doing at the game yesterday?" I shot back, calling her out on her **hypocrisy**.

"**Mocking** the cheerleaders," she said matter-of-factly, still spinning.

A shadow must have crossed my face as I thought of Marcy, because she stopped and put her hand over her mouth jokingly. "Oops. Forgot you're dating one of them."

"Not anymore," I said automatically.

---

impetuous: impulsive	**accentuating:** accenting	**hypocrisy:** deceitfulness
winsome: charming	**vapid:** dull	**mocking:** ridiculing

Winter smiled slowly. She skated back over to me and grabbed my arm as she jumped off her board. It skittered past us and into the fence. She rolled her big eyes up at me and smiled.

"You know, football star, if you want to ask me out, you should just ask," she said. This girl was not big on **pretense**.

My heart skipped a beat. I hadn't actually realized until that moment, with her looking at me in that teasing way, that I really did want to ask her out. It was **uncanny**. She could read my mind before I could. At first I wasn't sure whether it would be **expedient**, my being on the rebound and all. But why not? Marcy had already moved on. And besides, Winter was pretty, and funny, and athletic. Plus she was the exact opposite of Marcy, and at the moment, I had a **predilection** for girls who were nothing like my ex.

"All right. What are you doing Friday night?" I said.

"I got a hot date," Winter said, pushing herself up on her tiptoes and grinning. Her breath smelled like grape bubble gum. "With you."

---

pretense: posturing   **expedient:** worthwhile   **predilection:** preference
uncanny: strange

Chapter Three

"Oh, wow. I had *no* idea she would be there. Did you, Mike? Did you know she was going to be there?" Winter asked me in the darkened movie theater, at the top of her voice. "I mean, this movie is *so* **unconventional**! It is so unlike every other romantic comedy I have ever seen. Like, when he **spontaneously** fell over in the middle of the restaurant because his new shoes were *too* new? I did *not* see that coming!"

Winter was all sarcasm, all the time, and I was loving every minute of it. Unlike the rest of the audience, who clearly regarded her outbursts as **abrasive** rather than humorous. I slid down in my seat, trying to **stifle** my laughter as the people in front of us turned around, shushing Winter. A bunch more shot her irritated looks from all around the theater.

"Omigod! Who *likes* this excrement?" Winter said with a guffaw, as the protagonist wrapped his true love up in a romantic kiss.

"All right, you two. Now you're getting **profane**," the elderly gentleman behind us **upbraided** us. He gave me a **stern** look, like I was somehow Winter's **accomplice**. I didn't see how *excrement* was profane, but I shushed her anyway.

"Sorry. Sorry," Winter said, first to me, then to him, though her amused smile was anything but **penitent**. She hunkered down in her seat and ate a fistful of popcorn, and for a few minutes I thought she was actually done. In **hindsight**, that was a stupid assumption.

"The thing is, I love you," the guy on the screen said. *"Even if you are the most* **impertinent** *woman I know."*

unconventional: different	**upbraided:** reprimanded	**penitent:** regretful
spontaneously: impulsively	**stern:** serious	**hindsight:** retrospect
abrasive: irritating	**accomplice:** assistant (esp.	**impertinent:** rude
stifle: repress	in wrongdoing)	
profane: crude		

Winter laughed loudly. At least a dozen people turned around and scowled. The woman on the screen swooned and kissed the guy again.

"Oh, come on!" Winter shouted. "'I love you, even if you are the most impertinent woman I know'? He should get a slap for that line!"

Some woman stood up in the front of the theater. "Would you shut up already?"

Just then, a scrawny usher came in and knelt down next to Winter's aisle seat. He looked at me with **trepidation**—I was about three times his size—then directed his comments at Winter.

"Excuse me, Miss, but I'm afraid talking during the film is **prohibited**," he said, his Adam's apple bobbing up and down.

Winter adopted an innocent **façade**. "I wasn't talking."

The usher looked at me **skeptically** as the people behind us laughed and groaned. I shrugged. It wasn't as if I could **refute** his accusation. "I'm sorry, but I heard you myself," he said.

"Well I'm sorry that this movie sucks," Winter said.

I laughed. I couldn't help it. The usher looked like he just wanted to die. "I'm afraid I'm going to have to ask you to leave," he said. "Both of you."

"Are you kidding me? You're **banishing** me from the theater?" Winter said. "But I'm having so much fun!"

The usher looked at me imploringly. He was starting to sweat, and I could tell he was afraid I was going to start a fight, or at the very least make more of a scene than Winter already had.

"Maybe we should just go," I said to Winter, taking pity on this poor guy. After all, he was just trying to do his job.

"Yeah?" she asked, widening her eyes at me.

"Yeah. Let these people watch the rest of the movie. I'm starving anyway," I said. "Is there anyplace we can **procure** a burger around here?" I whispered to the usher.

---

trepidation: worry
prohibited: forbidden
façade: false appearance

skeptically: doubtfully
refute: deny

banishing: exiling
procure: obtain

He smiled in relief. Apparently my behavior was **atypical** of the situations he usually encountered around here.

"Most **expeditiously**, sir. Joe's Grill is just around the corner," he said **graciously**.

"Okay. If you want to bow to the Man, we'll bow to the Man," she stood up and handed the rest of her popcorn to the usher. "Have a snack on me."

I slid out of my seat and followed her up the aisle, to the tune of thunderous applause from the rest of the theater. Right before we got to the door, Winter turned around and curtseyed, and a few people laughed. So not everyone hated us. We were still cracking up when we hit the sidewalk.

"I gotta say, I've never been booted before," I told Winter.

"Really? Happens to me all the time," she said happily, pulling her velvet jacket closer to her.

"Why am I not surprised?" I asked, amused.

"I'm sorry. Are you mad? It's just that movie was *so* **prosaic**," she said.

"Actually, it was kind of cool. Getting kicked out, I mean," I said with pride.

"Yeah. You are such a badass now," she teased.

"Ha ha," I said flatly. "Anyway, I'm sorry you hated it. I thought girls liked romantic comedies."

"Well, you're not dealing with your average girl," she said, taking my hand.

I looked down at our entwined fingers, surprised. But in a good way. Winter was, hands down, the most **extroverted**, funny, unsettling girl I'd ever known. And I liked it.

"I'm getting that idea," I said.

Winter smiled slowly, then stood on her tiptoes and pulled me to her. It was the most intense kiss I had ever experienced. For the first time, I realized that there was no *way* I had been in love with Marcy.

---

atypical: unusual   **graciously:** politely   **extroverted:** outgoing
expeditiously: promptly   **prosaic:** unimaginative

Because even though she was hotter than hot, kissing her had never felt like this.

"And just for the record, I *do* like romantic comedies," she said when she pulled away.

"Wha?" I said, my head still swimming.

"I *love* them. I just love to **deride** them and laugh at them, that's all. I mean, did it not look like I was having fun in there?" she asked, arching one eyebrow.

I blinked. "Good point."

Winter laughed and grabbed both my hands, leaning back to pull me forward. "Come on. Let's go get you some food, football star," she teased.

I smiled and followed her down the street. Right then I would have followed her anywhere.

* * * * *

When I arrived at Ian's house for our regular Friday night game, there was an extra poker table set up in the basement, all **glossy** and new. The regular guys were there, but a couple of kids from the junior class were milling around as well, eating chips from a basket near the wall and looking around skittishly, like they were afraid someone was going to jump them and kick them out. I dropped my varsity jacket on the couch and slapped hands with Ian.

"What's with the new blood?" I asked.

"Well, I realized that having such a **finite** number of players was an unnecessary **hindrance** to my augmenting my income," Ian said **sagely**, putting on a businesslike **demeanor**. "So I thought I'd put the word out, get a few more people in. Besides, it might be good to **infuse** the game with some new energy."

"New meat, you mean," Chris said, joining the conversation and clapping Ian on the back. "This was the most **sagacious** move you've

---

deride: ridicule
glossy: sleek
finite: having an end

hindrance: obstacle
sagely: wisely
demeanor: outward manner

infuse: inject
sagacious: wise

ever made, man. We'll take these little losers for all they've got."

Ian and I both laughed. "Now, now, Chris. Let's not get too cocky," I joked. "Everyone here has an equal chance of winning."

Chris looked at me and scoffed, rolling his eyes. "Yeah, right. They wish."

He walked over to one of the juniors, took a chip right out of his hand, and popped it into his mouth. He stood there, chewing it in the kid's face, **goading** him. Luckily, the kid was smart enough to let it slide. This night was going to be interesting.

"All right, everyone, let's get started," Ian called out, taking his place as dealer at our usual table. Tyler, it seemed, had been tapped to run the new game—he took the seat of authority there. I settled in with Chris, Brad, and a couple of the new guys.

Ian dealt the hole cards, and I checked my draw. Five and three, suited. Not bad. Looked like I was going to have an **auspicious** night. Just as I was about to put in my first chips, the door to the basement opened, and everyone fell silent. For a split second, I'm sure we all thought we were snagged, but then our visitors stepped through the door, and everyone looked at me.

"'Sup?" Dominic Thomas asked, striding in like he owned the place. "Heard you got a poker game going."

There wasn't a guy in the room who didn't know what had gone on between me, Dominic, and Marcy. Even if you weren't a fan of the rumor mill, no one could have missed their stunningly inappropriate make-out sessions in the hallways all week long. As Dominic and his friends closed the door behind them, my jaw must have been on the floor. I was totally **flabbergasted**. What the hell was my number-one **adversary** doing here? Just the sight of him made my blood boil and got my adrenaline pumping. I felt like he was invading my private space, which just added insult to serious injury. This was my game. These were my friends. He had no business being here.

---

goading: prodding

auspicious: lucky
flabbergasted: shocked

adversary: enemy

Dominic took off his ever-present leather jacket and hung it carefully on one of the hooks near the door. His tight black T-shirt made him look like a total Gotti wannabe. What an extreme loser.

"So, where do we sit?" he asked, rubbing his hands together. His eyes fell on me, and his smile turned **rancorous**. As if *I'd* ever done anything to *him*. He had no reason to hate me, while I had every reason to get up from the table and kick his ass from here to the other side of town.

Ian looked at me, his expression full of **gravity**, and I knew that if I just said the word, he would dropkick Dominic and his friends out the door. But as I stared at Dominic, I was **overcome** with a new sentiment. I was going to wipe that smirk right off this kid's face.

"Sit here," I said **resolutely**.

The juniors at my table glanced at me **quizzically**, and I nodded at them. They got up **instantaneously** and moved to the wall to wait their turn. I even kicked a chair out for Dominic to take. As he sat down, the **acrimony** between us was palpable. I think everyone in the room was waiting for one of us to explode.

"Deal them in," I told Ian **nonchalantly**, tossing over my cards.

My friends did the same, and Ian shuffled the deck. I glanced sidelong at Dominic as he placed a toothpick in his mouth and started rolling it around. This asshole was going down.

* * * * *

An hour later, I had rendered Dominic Thomas completely **impotent**, and damn, was it fun. I can't place all the credit on my poker talent, though. The kid was so totally **inept** he made me and everyone else at the table look like the most **adept** players in the world. He wasn't particularly **cunning**. He fidgeted whenever he had a bad hand and leaned back in his seat whenever he was comfortable with his cards. Plus he was **oblivious** to everyone else's obvious tells. During

---

rancorous: hateful
gravity: seriousness
overcome: overwhelmed
resolutely: firmly
quizzically: curiously

instantaneously: instantly
acrimony: hatred
nonchalantly: casually
impotent: useless

inept: unskilled
adept: skillful
cunning: crafty
oblivious: unaware

one hand, Chris scratched the back of his neck about a hundred times—a clear sign of nervousness—but Dominic folded anyway and Chris took a twenty-five dollar pot on a pair of fours. Dominic looked like an idiot, and I wanted to hug Chris. Every time Dominic lost a pot, which was often, I **relished** the moment, no matter who had **acquired** his cash.

You stole my girlfriend, my friends and I are making off with all your money. Seems like an **equitable** *outcome to me*, I thought.

"Okay, everyone ante," Ian said as he shuffled the cards.

Some people play with big and little blinds and a rotating dealer, but in our games, Ian was always the dealer, so we had a regular ante. We each threw in two dollars worth of chips, then Ian dealt the cards. I glanced at Dominic as he checked his hole cards. He flinched, and I tried not to **exult**. This kid had a **pathetic** poker face. It made me wonder how he and Marcy had gotten away with their **subterfuge** for so long. Of course, I didn't want to think about that. I checked my own cards. Ian had dealt me a solid hand. A queen and a ten. I had a shot at a royal straight with these cards.

Over at the second table, one of the new kids cheered as he won a hand. Brad clucked his tongue and mucked his cards, pushing them toward Ian. Everyone else at my table called their bets. I expected Dominic to fold since he had a **paucity** of chips and was clearly holding some lame cards, but he threw in another two bucks. Apparently he was a **glutton** for punishment.

"Dealing the flop," Ian announced.

He placed three cards face up on the table, and it was all I could do to **quell** my excitement. There were the jack and king I needed, plus a useless two. All I needed in the next two communal cards was either a nine or an ace, and there was no way anyone could beat me.

One of Dominic's friends folded at this point, and Chris did as well. I upped the bet, and Dominic's other friend, Lucas, saw my bet. Much to my surprise, Dominic *raised* the bet.

---

relished: savored
acquired: taken
equitable: fair

exult: rejoice
pathetic: pitiful
subterfuge: deception

paucity: shortage
glutton: ready recipient
quell: quiet

"Wow. Someone must have some good cards," I **quipped**, glancing at Brad, who laughed. Normally, at this point, I might be getting a little nervous, wondering if I had misread my opponent. But Dominic was clearly sweating this one. He must have thought I was bluffing. Why, I have no idea. I had made sure to stay as still as possible all night long. It was amazing what having your sworn enemy at the table could do for your concentration.

"Whatever, dude," Dominic said.

"Dealing the turn," Ian said.

He flipped the card over on the table. It was a ten, which gave me a pair if the straight didn't work out. But it wasn't the strongest hand. Now I started to sweat a little, but there was no way I was dropping out. Call me **obstinate**, but Dominic was almost out of chips, and I wanted him out of here. Correction. I wanted to **debase** him, and *then* I wanted him out of here.

I threw in a couple more chips. Dominic looked at the pot in wonder, as if he wasn't expecting that move. Lucas saw my bet, then Dominic sighed and threw in two more chips.

"Everyone's in," Ian stated. "Dealing the river."

Please give me a nine or an ace, I begged silently. *Please give me a nine or an ace!*

Ian turned the last card over. I felt as if it were happening in slow motion, but then, there it was. The ace of spades.

Lucas groaned and threw his cards down. "You screwed me, O'Connor," he said.

"I guess that means you fold," Ian said dryly. "Mike?"

"I'm in," I said, adding two more chips.

We all looked at Dominic. He clenched his jaw and tossed his last chips into the pot. "I call," he said, and swallowed hard. "Whadaya got?" he asked.

As if *he* had anything good. I grinned, loving the moment, and placed my cards down on the table.

---

quipped: joked   obstinate: stubborn   debase: demean

"Holy crap!" Chris cried. "A straight, ace high!"

Dominic's skin turned waxy. He looked as if he might throw up all over the table.

"What do you have, Dom?" Lucas asked hopefully. Could none of these guys read body language?

"Pair of kings," he said, tossing his cards down.

"Better luck next time," I said, gathering up all the chips with **alacrity**. I had absolutely no **compassion** for Dominic. In fact, I couldn't have been more giddy if someone had just announced I'd won the MegaMillions jackpot. This win was the sweetest I could imagine.

Dominic threw his cards down and shoved his chair back. "We're outta here," he said to his friends. "Cash out."

He grabbed his leather jacket and stormed out the door without a second glance. Everyone except his two buddies laughed as the door slammed. A totally perfect end to a totally perfect night.

*   *   *   *   *

"Thanks for staying and helping me clean up," Ian said as I stacked the chips into their box.

"Are you kidding? I'm totally **indebted** to you, man," I said.

Ian laughed as he swept the coffee table by the couches free of Dorito crumbs. "Why? It's not like I **bilked** the guy on your behalf. You got the good cards, and you played like a pro."

"Thanks. And I know you didn't cheat. But I'm just saying, if it wasn't for you, there wouldn't be a game. And if there wasn't a game, I wouldn't have been able to rub Dominic's face in my total poker mastery," I said—somewhat **pretentiously**, I guess.

I'll admit it. I was living it up a little bit. So much of my irritation at Dominic and Marcy had been **alleviated** by tonight's many wins that I had a feeling I wouldn't even care if I saw him all over her

---

alacrity: eagerness
compassion: pity

indebted: owing gratitude
bilked: cheated

pretentiously: pompously
alleviated: eased

again in the hallway. Between my humiliation of the skeev, and my great date with Winter, I was feeling like myself again.

"'We're outta here! Cash out!'" I **imitated** Dominic, adding a whiney voice. "What a tool."

"Well, glad I could help," Ian said, tossing a bunch of cups and napkins in the trash. "I swear I had no idea he was coming."

"Whatever. I'm glad he did," I said. "I was happy to take the cocky bastard down a few pegs." I closed the chip box and snapped the latch. "In fact, it gave me a **notion**," I said in a leading way.

Ian paused. "Uh-oh. Why don't I like the sound of this?"

"What?" I replied innocently. "When have *I* ever come up with a bad scheme? That's usually *your* thing."

"You got me there," Ian said, pushing a couple of chairs in toward the new table. "So what's your idea?"

"Well, I was thinking . . . why don't we start up a second weekly game?" I said. "A high-stakes game."

"A high-stakes game," he repeated, his eyebrows raised. "The most **frugal** of my frugal friends wants me to start up a high-stakes game."

"Why not?" I said. "There's a **profusion** of wealth in this town. Why not use it to our advantage? We invite all the most **insipid** rich kids to the game and then **reap** the rewards."

Ian laughed and picked up the chip box to stow it in the cabinet. "You have one big night and all of a sudden you're a poker **prodigy** with **designs** on fleecing the upper class."

"Hey, don't **demonize** me," I said **defiantly**. "It was just a suggestion."

"I know. Chill," he said, walking over and leaning on the back of one of the chairs. "I'm not saying it's a bad idea. I'm all for greed as much as the next guy. I just don't want to make a rash decision. I mean, if all the guys come in here and start losing mad cash, they're going to think I'm **culpable**."

imitated: mimicked	**insipid:** dull	**demonize:** portray as evil
notion: idea	**reap:** harvest	**defiantly:** boldly
frugal: thrifty	**prodigy:** child genius	**culpable:** guilty
profusion: excess	**designs:** schemes	

"So we won't invite them all," I said. "Most of them wouldn't be able to buy in anyway."

Ian eyed me doubtfully, and I knew what he was thinking. That *I* couldn't really buy in either. I felt **agitated**, and my skin heated up.

"Don't worry about me," I said. "I'll just use this."

I emptied my pockets of all the cash I'd won from Dominic and his friends that night. It was definitely enough to get me into the first big game, at least. Slowly, Ian smiled.

"Come on," I said, knowing I had him. "We'll clean up."

"All right," he said finally. "I'm in."

agitated: nervous

Chapter Four

"Hey, man. So glad you guys invited me to this thing," Topher Ross said, dipping a tortilla chip into a vat of melted cheese. He flipped his long blond hair over his shoulder. "There's never anything to do around this stupid town."

Topher had just moved to New York from California the year before, and all we really knew about him was that he lived in one of the biggest houses in town and was absent from school at least once a week. Which, of course, made him mysterious and therefore coveted by all the ladies. He'd already dated most of the hottest chicks in school, which meant most of the guys hated him. But his obvious wealth qualified him for the game, and now that he was here for the game, he seemed like a pretty cool guy. I was actually kind of surprised Marcy hadn't set her sights on him instead of Dominic freakin' Thomas.

"I know," I said. I leaned back against the wall, clutching my cold soda. "Life around here is so **mundane**, we figured it'd be cool to try something new. It's gonna be fun."

I said this as much to convince myself as him. Now that we were all here, ready for the **seminal** high-stakes game, my heart was having a major fit. In fact, it had been **palpitating** all morning, ever since I had drained half my bank account so I could buy in and still have more money to play with.

"Damn right it's gonna be fun," Ian said, slapping me on the back. He took the wad of cash he had already collected and placed it inside the safe in one of the cabinets. I could practically see the dollar signs reflected in his eyes. "**Initiating** this game was the best idea you've ever had, Riley," he said over his shoulder as he locked the door.

---

mundane: ordinary
seminal: unprecedented

palpitating: throbbing

initiating: starting off, setting up

"Oh, dude. That's some **pungent** cheese!" Topher said with a grimace. He grabbed the soda right out of my hand and took a swig, washing his **rank** snack down.

"Uh . . . that's okay," I said, holding a hand up as he tried to give back my drink.

"Oh, sorry," he said. "I'll get ya another one."

Then he loped off toward the side table where the soda bottles and ice bucket sat, cutting through the rest of the crowd that had gathered in Ian's basement. All the wealthiest guys in school were there, bringing with them a **preponderance** of designer clothes, overpriced cologne, and state-of-the-art cell phones. Not to mention attitude. These guys had attitude coming out their *ears*. The **decibel** level was already staggering, and it only seemed to grow louder with each passing moment, as one guy after another vied for the attention of the group.

"Okay, I'm starting to think that maybe this wasn't the best idea," I said, glancing at the door behind me.

Ian's eyes widened. "Are you **intimating** that you want to leave?"

"Not intimating. I'm saying it flat out," I replied. "I think I should go."

"I'm **perplexed**," Ian said, a wrinkle appearing above his nose. "Wasn't this your idea?"

"I know, dude," I said, rolling my neck around. "It's just . . . ever since I took that money out of the bank this morning I've been kind of nervous."

"Don't think about the money." Ian placed his hand on my shoulder and squeezed, turning me to face the room. "Think about your total poker **hegemony** the other night. Think about how great it felt to knock those guys off their pedestals. You are going to **demolish** these suckers, relieve them of their **extraneous** cash! And it's going to feel *good*!"

"I don't know . . . ," I hedged.

---

pungent: strong smelling
rank: foul
preponderance: excessive number

decibel: loudness
intimating: implying
perplexed: baffled

hegemony: domination
demolish: destroy
extraneous: excess

"Besides, you heard what Topher said. We're performing a public service here," Ian told me.

I looked at him doubtfully.

"We're saving these guys from their **ennui**!" Ian announced.

I laughed. "You have a point there," I said. "But E, you know how hard I've worked to save up all this money. You know all the sacrifices I've made. Do I really want to risk losing half of it?"

"Okay. How about we **prescribe** a limit, then?" Ian suggested. "You can only bet half of what you brought with you."

I bit my lip and stared across the room at the **verdant** felt atop one of the poker tables. Ian's proposal did sound reasonable. Of course, I would be the one who would have to control myself. Something that was never all that easy in the heat of the game. But I had always managed to be responsible in the past. Now that there was more money on the line, I would just have to be *more* responsible.

"Come on. We're in this together, man. It wouldn't be the same without you. What do I have to do to **dissuade** you from leaving?" he asked.

"You could stop sounding like a used car salesman," I quipped.

"You're staying, aren't you?" Ian said.

I grinned. "Yeah, I'll stay."

"All right!" he slapped my hand just as the noise in the room reached a **crescendo**. The natives were getting restless. "Let's get this party started," Ian told me. "Get out there and work that poker **prowess**."

"I'll try," I said with a shrug.

Ian leveled me with a serious stare. "Do or do not. There is no try."

*   *   *   *   *

I'm not usually **inclined** to underestimate my opponents, but an hour later, if anyone had asked me, I would have said with absolute

---

ennui: boredom
prescribe: specify
verdant: green

dissuade: advise against
crescendo: climax

prowess: great ability
inclined: predisposed

certainty that the guys I was playing were not only **sophomoric**, but **hapless**. And that would have been *kind*. Not only did they seem to know zip about Texas Hold 'Em and the probability of winning on certain hands, but they were getting *no* cards. Half of them folded right after the flop, and I just kept taking pot after undefended pot. In my usual game, that would mean **moderate** winnings, but in this game, with higher minimum bets, I was cleaning up. And it took almost no effort!

This *was* the best idea I had ever had!

"**Kudos**, dude," Topher said as I gathered up my latest pile of chips. "You're like the poker guru."

"Thanks, man," I said with a smile.

Dominic's friend Lucas was more **truculent**. "Whatever. You're just having a lucky night."

"Kind of like the *other* night when I kicked your and Dominic's asses?" I asked, stacking my chips in twenty-five-dollar **increments**. "Was I lucky then, too?"

Lucas blew out a breath and shook his head. He sunk lower in his seat, staring down at the table.

"Where is Dominic tonight, anyway?" Ian asked. "Still licking his wounds?"

I laughed, and Ian and I exchanged a look. Maybe we were rubbing it in a little, but hell, that was half the fun. Maybe more, this time.

"How about we take a break before the next hand?" Ian suggested, shuffling the cards.

"I gotta take a piss anyway," Lucas said, shoving back from the table before stalking out of the room.

"I think I'm really developing a **rapport** with that guy," Ian **deadpanned**.

I cracked up laughing as everyone else made off for the snack table or the bathroom. Ian eyed my chips.

"So, feeling a little more **sanguine** about tonight?" he asked.

---

sophomoric: childish	**truculent:** savage	**deadpanned:** said matter-
hapless: unfortunate	**increments:** increased	of-factly
moderate: mediocre	amounts	**sanguine:** confident
kudos: praise	**rapport:** personal	
	connection	

"Yeah, you bet your ass I am," I said. "And I have your **laudatory** comments to thank for it, brotha," I added, slapping him on the back.

"Please. I knew your **empirical** knowledge of the game would make you outclass these losers any day," Ian said, lifting his shoulders. "They probably learned everything they know from *Celebrity Poker Showdown.*"

"No doubt," I said, feeling quite pleased with myself.

"So how much you up?" he asked.

I looked over the chips and quickly estimated my winnings. "I think I've tripled my money," I said incredulously.

"No way," Ian replied, wide-eyed. "See? You were all worried about your bank account, but now it's going to be **replete** with cash."

My heart thumped as I stared at the **ornate** design on top of the professional chips Ian had sprung for. "Yeah."

"What's the matter now?" Ian asked. "Winner's remorse?"

"No," I said. "No. It's just . . . how am I going to explain the sudden influx of money to my parents?"

Ian blinked. Neither one of us had thought of this. "Well, better than explaining a sudden **dearth**, right?"

"Good point," I replied.

Still, as the other guys returned to the table, I was feeling a strong **inclination** to quit while I was ahead. That was my usual M.O. anyway, and now that I realized that my new income was going to render me suspect, I was even more inclined to bail. I had never told my parents about our poker games, not even the little ones. In their eyes, risking money was an **egregious** crime. But before, I never had trouble hiding it—anything I won was silly pocket money. This kind of cash was going to be a lot harder to stow.

"I think I'm gonna cash out," I announced, once everyone was seated.

---

laudatory: praising
empirical: based on experience
replete: full

ornate: excessively decorated
dearth: shortage

inclination: desire
egregious: flagrant

"Cool, dude," Topher replied, while another guy, Jonah, slapped my hand amicably.

"What? You've gotta be *kidding* me," Lucas protested.

A couple of the other guys grumbled as well. Talk about a **divisive** announcement. Everyone looked at Lucas, uncomfortable.

"Come on, man," Lucas said, sitting up straight and raising his palms on the table. I found myself hoping he had washed them after doing his business. "You gotta at least give us a chance to win *some* of our money back."

"Yeah," one of the other guys chorused. "Don't be a wank."

"A *greedy* wank," Lucas amended.

I looked around at their pleading, challenging expressions and felt myself start to **oscillate**. Normally, I'm fairly **obdurate** in these situations, but in that moment, I felt kind of sorry for them. They didn't know what the hell they were doing, and I had taken advantage of that. Besides, if I lost a little money back, I would still be up, they would be **placated**, and it would be less cash to explain to my parents.

I settled back down and nodded to Ian. "All right. Deal me in."

*   *   *   *   *

Big mistake. Huge, awful, horrible, horrifying mistake. An hour later my winning streak had **stagnated**. Not just stagnated, but reversed itself. My pile of chips had been all but **effaced**. I was losing. Big time. On every hand. The cards were not there. And as the guys around me grew more and more relaxed, I grew more and more **disheartened**. Why had I let them **exhort** me to play more hands? Why had I let Ian convince me to stay in the first place?

Of course, there was one little misstep that I couldn't blame on anyone but myself—the fact that I had broken my own rule. I had dipped in to my extra chips—the ones Ian and I had decided that I

---

divisive: dividing   **placated:** appeased   **disheartened:** discouraged
oscillate: waver   **stagnated:** gone stale   **exhort:** urge strongly
obdurate: inflexible   **effaced:** erased

wouldn't touch. I was fairly sure that Ian hadn't even realized that I made this **illicit** move, that the few chips I had left represented, in fact, the last of my money.

If I didn't win this hand, I would be screwed. So very, very screwed.

"So, whadaya say, Riley?" Lucas asked, grinning. "One more hand. I believe you've only got the cash for one more hand."

I stared at the **wily** bastard, wishing I could **incinerate** him with my eyes, Superman style. It was his fault—his fault I was still there, his fault I was down. I could have walked out of here a winner, but he had goaded me into staying. Well, I couldn't back down now. I still had one more shot, and I wasn't going to let this jerk run me out of here.

"Sure," I said **genially**. "One more hand."

"You sure about that, man?" Ian asked.

"Just deal me in," I said through my teeth. I knew it was probably a **fatuous** decision, but I didn't need my best friend calling me on it.

Ian did as I said. As I pulled my hole cards to me, I said a little prayer. It didn't work. I had a two and a queen, unsuited. Not that it mattered. What the hell was I going to do with a two and a queen?

"You folding, Riley?" Lucas teased.

I made my face **impassive**, even though inside I was a **maelstrom** of doubt, guilt, and fear. I picked up a couple of chips and threw them in.

"What the hell," I said, lifting a shoulder.

The second my chips were in the pot I wanted to **retract** the bet. What was I doing? Did I think I was invincible or something? I mean, this night had proven the exact opposite. Had I lost my mind? At least if I held on to the few chips I had I would be walking out with *something*. At this point it would be a miracle if I didn't go bust.

I glanced **furtively** at Ian as he dealt the flop.

Gimme a miracle here, buddy. Give me anything, I thought.

---

illicit: unlawful
wily: sly
incinerate: burn

genially: in a friendly manner
fatuous: foolish
impassive: expressionless

maelstrom: storm
retract: take back
furtively: secretly

The flop was a ten, a two, and a king. I had a pair of twos. Total suckage.

But Topher and Jonah both folded, good sign. Maybe *everyone* had crap cards.

The fifth guy at the table, Thomas something or other, threw in two chips. I took a deep breath. Lucas watched me carefully. My stack of chips was pathetic. I had already lowered myself into the **quagmire**. My sole hope of redeeming myself was to somehow win this hand. And I did have a shot. With a queen I could pull out two pair. Or maybe even a full house. I looked at Lucas and my pride won out over my logic. I saw Thomas's bet.

Lucas tapped his foot under the table as he considered. A feeling of sudden hope **permeated** my soul. This was a classic tell. He was nervous. He didn't have the cards. He took a deep breath and saw my bet.

"Dealing the turn," Ian said.

It was a queen. I had to concentrate to keep from sitting up a bit straighter. I had my two pair, and if the poker gods were smiling on me, I might even have a shot at a full house.

Thomas folded. It was between me and Lucas. Feeling slightly more confident, I threw in a couple more chips. It was a decent pot. If I could take it, I would be back in the game.

"Like you said, what the hell," Lucas said. He tossed in two more chips, seeing my bet and barely making a dent in his winnings. "Let's see that river," he said to Ian.

Ian looked at me. We were all holding our breath. In my mind I could hear the death **knell** sounding. What were the chances that one of the two queens was still in his hand, let alone sitting atop the deck? If I wasn't so nervous, I might have been able to figure out the math, but as it was, you couldn't even have **elicited** the answer to 2 + 2 from my brain.

"Dealing the river," Ian said.

---

quagmire: difficult position   **knell:** announcing sound   **elicited:** drawn forth
permeated: seeped through

He turned the card over. The queen of hearts.

Yes! I thought. *Full house.*

I threw in my last two chips. I was back in the game, baby.

"I call," Lucas said, placing his bet. "What do you have?"

"Full house," I said triumphantly, standing up as I threw my cards down. "Queens over twos." God, it felt good. I was still so, so, so down, but at least I had been granted a **reprieve**. "Whadaya got?" I asked Lucas. Like it mattered.

Slowly, ever so slowly, Lucas's mouth twisted into a **wry**, victorious grin, and just like that, I hit the **nadir** of my short existence.

"Full house," he said. "*Kings over queens.*"

He stood up and placed his two kings down on the table. The room spun as he and his buddies cheered **mercilessly**. Lucas had totally schooled me. His foot tapping wasn't a tell but a **flagrant ruse** that I should have seen coming from a mile away. It was all part of the game. He had beaten me fair and square. I looked at the empty space of felt in front of me—the space where much of my life savings had once been.

"Hey, man. It's gonna be all right," Ian said, stepping up next to me.

"No, it's not," I said. "It is *so* not going to be all right."

I appreciated his effort, but as of that moment, I was **inconsolable**. As of that moment, my life was over.

*   *   *   *   *

I sat outside on the front steps of my house for a long time, feeling **morose** and dejected, wondering what the hell I was going to do next. It was a cool October evening, and a **tranquil** breeze rustled the leaves in the trees on our front lawn. I took a deep breath, hoping it would clear my head. Fall was my favorite time of year, and I normally loved this type of weather. It meant football and pep rallies and parties. I usually found it energizing. But tonight I couldn't

reprieve: delay of punishment	**mercilessly:** unrelentingly	**inconsolable:** beyond being comforted
wry: ironically humorous	**flagrant:** obvious	**morose:** gloomy
nadir: lowest point	**ruse:** trick	**tranquil:** calm

have felt more **lethargic**. The very idea of walking into my house exhausted me.

My parents were in the living room, watching TV, oblivious to the **reprehensible transgression** their son had just committed. I couldn't **disclose** to them what I had done. Just imagining the looks of disappointment they would throw at me made me sick to my stomach. My flagrant disregard for their rules, for their beliefs, would crush them. I had always been the **paradigm** of the perfect son—working hard, getting good grades, succeeding at sports. I had never given them a single reason to have a **modicum** of doubt in me. And now, in one night, I had killed all that.

I had to find a way to fix this before they got our bank statements and saw the **discrepancy** between this one and the last. And until I did, keeping the secret from my parents was **paramount**.

I took a deep breath, forced myself to stand up, and went inside. There they were, cuddled up together on the couch. The scenario was so **placid** and normal, it almost didn't make sense to my off-kilter brain. My mom looked up from the TV when she saw my shadow.

"Hi, Michael! Did you have fun at Ian's?" she asked.

"Yeah," I said automatically. "We just hung out with some of the guys. Nothing big."

I couldn't believe how **lucid** I was, considering that my life was flashing before my eyes. I was supposed to **venerate** my parents, not **deceive** them right to their faces. Maybe I should just tell them. Maybe they would be **lenient**. Maybe they wouldn't hate me. But even as I thought about it, I knew it was a risk I wasn't willing to take.

"Are you okay, son?" my father asked. "You look kind of pale."

"Actually, I think I ate too much junk food," I told them. "I think I'm just gonna go to bed."

"Okay. I'll come in and check on you in a little while," my mom said with a smile.

---

lethargic: sluggish	**paradigm:** typical example	**lucid:** clearheaded
reprehensible: unforgiveable	**modicum:** small portion	**venerate:** revere
transgression: violation	**discrepancy:** disagreement	**deceive:** mislead
disclose: reveal	**paramount:** all-important	**lenient:** permissive
	placid: calm	

"Thanks, Mom," I said.

Then I turned toward the hallway and got out of there before I could break down. Back in my room, I closed the door and lay down on my bed, staring up at the ceiling with my fists at my temples. My breath was short and panicked. What had I done? What was I going to do? I had no ideas. Zilch. Zero. Nada.

I took a deep breath and tried to force myself to chill. I needed to calm down and think. It was just one **digression**. I would fix it. I had to. I just had to attack this problem with the **fervency** with which I had attacked every other obstacle in my life.

Unfortunately, I had no idea where to begin.

digression: deviation   **fervency:** enthusiasm

As I walked into school on Thursday morning, I was barely **cognizant**. I hadn't slept at all, and even though my heart was pounding as if I'd just run ten miles, my brain was all fuzzy and exhausted. I felt like I had sucked down ten cups of super-caffeinated coffee, then followed it up with a sleeping pill. My body had no idea what to do with itself.

In the front hall, a bunch of my teammates were **cavorting** around with a football, tossing it back and forth and playing a mini game. A dozen girls stood against the walls, giggling and throwing out flirtatious glances. Two days ago I would have joined in the game, but this morning the whole thing seemed so **inane** to me. I was not in an **ebullient** mood.

"Mike! Catch!" Tim Brittan called out, lobbing the ball in my direction. I caught it, tossed it **languidly** back to him, and kept walking.

"What's the matter, man?" one of the guys called after me.

"Not now," I said. I guess when I was exhausted and guilt-ridden, I also became **laconic**. I was learning all kinds of things about myself lately. Unfortunately, none of it was good.

As I approached my locker, I saw that Winter was waiting for me. Just the sight of her cheered me up considerably. She looked adorable in a plaid miniskirt and denim jacket **embellished** with rhinestones, country-western style. There was no doubt that Winter Dumas walked to the beat of her own drummer.

"Hey!" I said with a small smile.

But my happiness was **ephemeral**. Winter did not look pleased. Cute maybe, but not pleased.

---

cognizant: aware
cavorting: frolicking
inane: silly

ebullient: enthusiastic
languidly: lazily
laconic: mysteriously quiet

embellished: enhanced
ephemeral: short-lived

"Not that I want to be the ball-breaking girlfriend after one date, but weren't you supposed to call me last night?" she asked, leaning her shoulder against the locker next to mine. I looked at her blankly. All I could remember about last night was my spectacular downward spiral. "We were going to watch *Invasion* together?" she prompted.

"Oh, God," I said, rolling my eyes closed. "I am *so* sorry. I got home later than I thought I would from Ian's, and I just . . ."

I was **bereft** of excuses. I should have called her anyway. I just—

"Forgot," she supplied with a smirk. "So I'm forgettable. That's cool. It's good to know, actually. Maybe I should consider getting a boob job. It's too late to grow long legs, but . . ."

I laughed. "Very funny," I said. "You do any of that, and I'll never speak to you again."

"Wouldn't be much of a change," she said with an overly dramatic sigh.

Her words may have sounded like a **rebuke**, but I could tell from her expression that she wasn't actually mad. Winter was not the ball-and-chain type of girl. She was just messing with me. But I felt bad anyway. Even more so because instead of talking to her, which would have been fun, I had been busy losing all my money like an idiot. Why hadn't I just stayed home and kept my phone date? If only I could go back in time. That was exactly what I would do.

"I'm sorry. I really am," I said, leaning forward and placing my forehead against the cool metal of the locker. "I'm such an asshole."

"All right, all right. Don't go all drama queen on me now," Winter joked. "You're forgiven."

I took a deep breath and blew it out, wishing there was something I could do to calm my pulse, to stop the bile from rolling around in my gut.

---

bereft: deprived   **rebuke:** reprimand

"Hey," she said, turning serious. "Are you okay? Mike?"

I looked down into her concerned green eyes and felt even worse yet. Little did she know she was dating a total moron who couldn't even hold on to his own cash.

You are a total loser, I chided myself. *You don't deserve a girl this cool.*

"I'm fine," I told her. And then I was saved by the first bell. "I'd better get to class."

I opened my locker, grabbed a few books, and then slammed it. Hard.

"Okay," she said. "But later, at lunch, you'll tell me what's wrong."

"Yeah. Okay," I said quickly, dismissively. "We'll talk at lunch."

Then I gave her a dry kiss on the cheek and ran off to class on the other side of the school. I walked through the door just as the second bell rang.

"Mr. Riley! Nice of you to join us," Mr. Weeks, my history teacher, greeted me with his wrinkled face set in its usual, **dour** expression.

The second I saw what he was doing, I wanted to **abscond** from the school and never look back. He was placing papers face down on everyone's desks. We hadn't recently *taken* a quiz, so that had to mean—

"Pop quiz!" he announced, placing the last paper on my empty desk at the front of the room. "Hope you all did your reading last night!"

I dropped into my chair, relieving my now quaking legs, and pulled out a pen. What had I been thinking? Mr. Weeks was **notorious** for his pop quizzes, but we hadn't had one all year. Of course he would give one on the morning after I had completely skipped my homework for the first time ever. Usually, I was so **fastidious** about my work that even my parents urge me to take breaks. Now there was

---

dour: harsh
abscond: leave secretly

notorious: unfavorably well-known

fastidious: picky

going to be a huge **blemish** on my record, and Mr. Weeks was going to peg me as **indolent** and irresponsible for the rest of the year.

"You have thirty minutes to complete the quiz," Mr. Weeks said, sitting down behind his **commodious** desk. "Turn your papers over . . . now."

There was a rustling of pages, and then everyone set to work. Pencils and pens scratched all around me, but as I ran my eyes down the list of questions, my **compunction** was compounded. I didn't know a single answer. Not one thing looked familiar. Oh yeah. Weeks was going to be **lavishing** me with praise after this performance.

I decided to start with the multiple-choice section and just start guessing. Maybe, just maybe, I would be luckier today than I had been last night.

*   *   *   *   *

By the time lunch rolled around, I was a wreck. All I could think about all morning was my bank account, the balance that used to be there, and the balance that was there now. What my parents would do once the situation had been **elucidated**. That was the worst part—thinking about how disappointed they were going to be. I needed to talk to someone. I needed to confess and maybe even get **absolution**. But since there was no priest on campus, and I wasn't that religious anyway, I decided to take Winter on as my new **confidant**. It made perfect sense. I couldn't tell Ian that I had lost the bank. I was too ashamed. And besides, Winter was so different from everyone else I knew, maybe she would have a different perspective. Maybe she could come up with a solution I hadn't even thought of yet. Like, I don't know, selling a kidney or something.

I took her outside to the picnic tables at lunch. It was a sunny fall day, and even though there was a cool breeze in the air, the sun

---

blemish: taint
indolent: lazy
commodious: spacious
compunction: guilt

lavishing: heaping on
elucidated: made clear
absolution: forgiveness

confidant: one to tell
secrets to

was strong enough to keep us warm. Winter's skin was **luminous** in that light, and I just wished we could sit out there and talk about something easy, or even make out a little—do something normal. But I had pretty much killed that possibility with my flash of irresponsibility. There was no normal for me today.

So instead I spilled out the whole awful story. Winter was great, unsurprisingly. She listened attentively throughout the sordid tale, but when I finally got to the actual amount of money I'd lost, she **balked**. In fact, I think she almost choked on her bagel.

"Are you kidding me?" she asked, sucking down some soda to clear her throat. "Please tell me you're kidding."

Okay, I hadn't expected her to be happy for me, but I also didn't expect her to look at me like I was some kind of **nefarious** fiend. It was my money I had lost, after all, not hers.

"No. I'm not kidding," I said **brusquely**. "That's why they call it a high-stakes game."

"Damn," she said under her breath. Then she saw my face and shrugged, smiling apologetically. "Sorry. I'm just **penurious** by nature. I can't even imagine taking out that much money, let alone gambling it."

I squirmed, feeling sick to my stomach. I knew she hadn't meant to rub it in, but that was exactly what she had done. I pushed my cafeteria-issue pizza away from me, no longer wanting to stare at the slowly **congealing** cheese.

"Well, thanks for your **candor**, I guess," I said. I knew she was right, of course. That's why I felt so horrible.

"So . . . what are you going to do?" she asked sympathetically.

"Not a clue," I said. "Any ideas?"

"Sell a kidney?" she suggested.

I laughed half-heartedly. How had I known she was going to say that?

"Maybe you should tell your parents," she suggested.

•

luminous: glowing	**brusquely:** bluntly	**congealing:** becoming solid
balked: stopped short	**penurious:** stingy	**candor:** honesty
nefarious: wicked		

"No. I can't do that," I said firmly.

"Why? You don't know. They might be totally understanding about it," she replied.

"No. It's not an option," I said. "They would never look at me the same way again."

Winter eyed me with obvious pity. This conversation wasn't going as well as I had hoped it would. I wanted her to offer her **condolences**, make me feel better. But now it was clear that there was no way to make me feel better about a mistake I had already made.

"I'm just gonna have to win it back," I said, taking a sip of my soda.

"Oh, yeah. *There's* a good plan," she said sarcastically.

"What? It could work," I replied.

"Uh, maybe it would be better if you just **capitulate** to lady luck," Winter suggested. "You know, quit while you're *not* ahead. At least you still have *some* money in the bank. If you play and lose, you could end up with nothing."

"Okay, I see your point. And it's a **judicious** argument," I told her. "But it's a chance I'm going to have to take."

"Why?" she asked.

"Have you not been listening to me?" I asked, my voice rising. "My parents are going to kill me."

"First of all, no they're not. They're not actually going to *kill* you. They may be disappointed, but they're not going to take the life of their one and only son," she said flatly. "Secondly, do you not see how **fraught** with flaws this plan is? Let's say, **hypothetically**, you go over to Ian's and play a few hands. You win a couple and you're up a little, but not enough. So you start betting a little more, playing a little more dangerously. Then all you've got to do is lose one big hand and you're back where you started. Or worse."

Wow. She was really launching a **polemic** here.

"Your confidence in me is heartening. Really," I said.

---

condolences: sympathies
capitulate: give in
judicious: wise

fraught: full
hypothetically: theoretically

polemic: aggressive verbal attack

"Mike—"

"I'm not going to lose it all back," I told her.

"Oh, so now you're **clairvoyant** all of a sudden?" she asked. "Now you know exactly what cards you're going to be dealt?"

The girl did not want me to play.

"Well, if I'm dealt bad cards, I'll fold," I told her.

"You still lose money when you fold," she pointed out.

Even in the midst of this argument and my tension, I was impressed that she knew anything about poker. I really did like this girl. Too bad I met her right when my life was totally falling apart. I took a deep breath and leaned forward.

"Look, this is the only choice I have," I told her. "I have to put that money back before my parents realize it's gone. I just have to."

Winter looked at me for a long moment, and I wondered if she was going to get up and walk away and never look back. But instead, she dropped back in her chair, popped a piece of bagel into her mouth, and shrugged.

"Well, then. I guess I wish you luck."

*   *   *   *   *

That Friday night I sat at my regular poker game with my friends, my leg bouncing up and down under the table as I waited for Brad to make his bet. The table was silent, and tension gripped the room. Both my fault. I had been **caustic** and impatient ever since I walked in, two things that didn't exactly **engender camaraderie**. This was supposed to be a fun game, a casual thing, but tonight I had turned it into a war.

"Dude. Are you going to bet, ever?" I said flatly.

Brad shot me a look of death. "Whatever," he said, tossing in a couple of chips.

"Good. I see your bet, and I raise you," I said, throwing in.

---

clairvoyant: possessing a sixth sense

caustic: scathing
engender: produce

camaraderie: brotherhood

"Uh, Mike?" Ian said. "You can't raise the bet ten dollars. There's a two-dollar limit, remember?"

I laughed. "Right. I forgot this wasn't the *real* game," I said.

Ian's face turned to stone. I knew he was annoyed that I had **alluded** to the high-stakes game, which these guys hadn't been invited to. But we had made that decision together, knowing they were too **impecunious** to afford it. Still, that didn't change the fact that now *I* was in the poor house. I needed money, and at that moment I didn't care where it came from. **Avarice** had taken over. Well, that and fear.

"Come on, Brad. Be a man," I said. "There isn't even any real money in that pot yet."

"Yeah, well, my **diminutive** paycheck begs to differ," Brad said, throwing his cards down. "I fold."

He shoved away from the table, got up, and grabbed his jacket.

"What's your problem, man?" I asked, standing as well. "When did you become so **irascible**?"

"Me?" Brad shot back, shoving his arms into his jacket. "I don't even know who the hell you are, man. You've been more **mercurial** tonight than my girlfriend at that time of the month."

I snorted a laugh and looked at the other guys. They all avoided my gaze. Suddenly I felt a pit of guilt start to form in my stomach. What was wrong with me?

"Come on, man," I said, fighting for **equanimity**. "Don't go. I'm sorry, all right? I'll stop being an ass."

Brad took a deep breath. "I'm just not in the mood, Mike. I'm not gonna stick around and wait for you to **denigrate** me again or . . . or **instigate** another showdown. You know, this used to be fun."

Talk about a drama queen. "You know what? Fine. If you wanna go, go. Don't let me **deter** you," I snapped.

I sat down and pulled my winnings toward me, stacking up the few chips I could now call my own. Brad turned around and

---

alluded: hinted	**irascible**: hot-tempered	**denigrate**: belittle
impecunious: penniless	**mercurial**: unpredictable	**instigate**: provoke
avarice: greed	**equanimity**: composure	**deter**: discourage
diminutive: small		

slammed the door on his way out. I could feel everyone staring at me, and I started to sweat.

"So, you gonna deal or what?" I snapped at Ian.

"Dude, what's wrong with you?" Tyler asked.

"Not you too, Brooks," I said.

"Mike, maybe you should **abstain** from this next hand," Ian suggested. "Or the next couple. Take a break and chill for a little bit."

My eyes flashed. "What are you, now? My mother?" I asked. The second I said it, I wanted to take it back. I couldn't believe how **belligerent** I was acting. But I guess that's what sheer panic can do to you. "Deal me in," I said quietly, tossing my two chips into the pot.

Ian sighed, looked around at Chris and Brad, and dealt the cards. I pulled my two hole cards to me and checked them. Two fours. A promising start. We all placed our bets.

"Dealing the flop," Ian said. He sounded tired. Maybe even a little wary.

In the flop were a ten, a queen, and a two. Nothing that could even remotely help me. The best I could do now was three of a kind or, if lady luck was smiling on me, four of a kind. Brad threw in his bet. Chris raised it. Now I either had to see his raised bet or fold.

My heart pounded in my ears. I should have listened to Ian and sat this one out. Now I could either bluff and pray or fold and give up half of what I had already won. Which wasn't much. Holding my breath, I decided to throw **prudence** out the window. I saw Chris's bet.

Ian blew out a sigh. "Dealing the turn," he said.

He turned the card over. Another ten. Okay. This was good. Now I had two pair with my two fours and the two tens on the table. Now I could even pull out a full house, potentially.

We all put in our bets. Chris raised again. I saw his bet. A trickle of sweat ran down my cheek from my temple.

"Dealing the river," Ian said.

---

abstain: not partake   **belligerent:** hostile   **prudence:** good judgment

He turned over the card. A king. I had to hope my two pair was the best hand out there.

We all placed our final bets.

"What's everybody got?" Ian asked.

"Two pair," Tyler said. "Tens and twos."

Yes! I had *him* beat.

"Two pair. Tens and fours," I said triumphantly.

Everyone looked at Chris. He seemed almost sorry as he turned over the winning hand. "I got a straight," he said. "Ace high."

I gulped. There were the cards. He had a jack and an ace in the hole, plus the ten, queen, and king on the table. He leaned forward and dragged all the chips in the pot toward him and it took every ounce of **fortitude** I could muster to keep from breaking down. I was down to my last two chips. Two measly dollars from the hundred I had taken out, hoping to double it and put a dent in what I had already lost. Everyone at the table looked at me in pity and with maybe a little bit of fear, wondering if I was going to explode again. But I didn't have any explosions left in me. It was one of the most **ignominious** moments of my life, and all I wanted to do was crawl home with my tail between my legs.

*   *   *   *   *

I left after that last game and went home in an **abject** condition. I couldn't believe I had lost even *more* money. The situation was officially **exigent**. Unless some **magnanimous benefactor** suddenly swooped in from on high with a huge check or some unknown wealthy relative died and **bequeathed** his estate to me, I was in serious trouble.

My parents were out to dinner, so at least I had the house to myself to wallow in my **despondency**. I walked into my room and closed the door quietly behind me. I sat down on the edge of my bed

fortitude: strength	**exigent:** demanding action	**benefactor:** donor
ignominious: humiliating	**magnanimous:** good-hearted	**bequeathed:** endowed
abject: spiritless		**despondency:** hopelessness

and looked at the clock. It was 10 P.M. Football curfew had started. The night stretched out in front of me like a tunnel of torture. I knew that there would be no sleep, that I would toss and turn all night thinking about what I had done, and that if I didn't sleep soon I would tank in the game tomorrow. One night of high-stakes gambling, and I had ruined everything. Why had I ever come up with that stupid idea?

I had to chalk it all up to ego. It had felt so good to take Dominic down that I had wanted to experience that high again. Little did I know I was setting myself up for the exact opposite. This was the lowest of lows. And it was **interminable**.

With a sigh, I stood up and slipped out of my varsity jacket. I flipped my computer on to check my email, maybe distract myself for a little while. Right after I typed in my password, a pop-up add appeared on my screen. I automatically went to close it—I have a particular **aversion** to those annoying ads—but my finger froze, hovering over the mouse.

PokerParty.com! Be a winner! it read.

There it was. A perfect **presage**. Just when I was floundering for a way out, a way out appeared.

My heart started to pound, and my palms were instantly bathed in sweat. Online poker. Of course. I didn't have to wait for the Wednesday and Friday night games to win back my money. And I didn't have to feel like I was fleecing my friends. These things were available 24/7 with strangers from around the world putting up their cash.

But they're dangerous, a little voice in my mind told me. *Because they're available all the time, you can also* lose *all the time.*

But even as I thought this, I found myself clicking on the link. I was under **duress** here, and I was ready to grab at any life-preserver thrown my way. I took a deep breath as I was welcomed in to the colorful website. It looked pretty cool. The minimum bets were

---

interminable: endless   **presage:** omen   **duress:** threat
aversion: dislike

nominal, so I could be **circumspect** while feeling out the situation. Besides, I bet a lot of the people playing on this site had never even played before. I would be an expert among a **plethora** of **novices**. All in all, it seemed like the perfect way to get ahead on my debt.

I clicked the "Sign Up" button and read through the steps **entailed** in becoming a member. I had to be 21, of course, but that was easy enough to fudge. I had my check card with my name on it, which also happened to be my father's name. The benefits of being a "junior." Both of our names were on my bank account as well, so they had no way of knowing I wasn't Michael Senior. Feeling **intrepid** and in control for the first time since Wednesday night, I quickly signed up. Before I knew it, I was creating a screen name—"Mikey_Sr," just for good measure—and I was welcomed into a game.

I took a deep breath as the "dealer" asked me to place my first bet. The good thing about this was there were no distractions. No one around me being **obstreperous** or irksome. The bad thing was **legerdemain** would be much easier—not just for me, but for everyone. I wouldn't be able to see anyone's tells or read their eyes, which was a big part of the game. But I figured that as long as I was **diligent** and paid attention, I could come out on top.

I clicked on the mouse and placed my first bet.

---

nominal: insignificant
circumspect: cautious
plethora: abundance
novices: beginners

entailed: involved
intrepid: adventurous
obstreperous: noisy

legerdemain: sleight of hand
diligent: dedicated

Saturday morning was our away game against Washington High. I was so exhausted as I boarded the bus with my teammates, I **contemplated abdicating** my quarterback position to the backup, Charlie Warner. He would clearly do a much better job than I would. I might have done it if I didn't know for sure that Coach would hunt me down and skin me alive. This was an important game against one of the most **redoubtable** opponents on our schedule. I had to be there, as much as my brain was somewhere else—on my computer, to be exact.

I had been up half the night playing at PokerParty.com. With each game I started, I told myself it was the last one, but then I would be up a bit and my adrenaline would take over, wanting to win more. If I was suddenly down, I knew I couldn't log off because I had to win my money back. Neither winning nor losing could **induce** me to turn off the damn computer. And now I was paying the price. I was yawning like mad, my head was all muddled, and all I could think about was getting through the damn game so I could get home and start betting again.

I was an **execrable** human being.

As Coach gathered us together in Washington High's visitor locker room for his weekly pre-game **oration**, I sat at the back of the crowd, sucking down my second Red Bull of the morning. I ducked behind some of the bigger linemen, trying to **elude** the coach's attention. He wasn't big on caffeine, always telling us it was **deleterious** to our training and would stunt our growth. Unfortunately, today I would be useless without it.

contemplated: thought about
abdicating: giving up
redoubtable: formidable
induce: cause
execrable: detestable
oration: speech
elude: evade
deleterious: harmful

"All right everyone, let's remember the game plan," Coach said. "Their run game is for crap and they know it, so what are they gonna do?"

"They're gonna throw, Coach," Tim shouted.

"Damn right. That's all they're gonna do," Coach said. "So what're *we* gonna do?"

"Blitz!" the team shouted.

"That's right! We're gonna pressure them! Bronson! I expect to see at least two sacks out of you today, you got me?"

"Yes, Coach!" Bronson replied.

I yawned hugely, hiding my gaping mouth behind my hand. Out on the field Washington High's marching band started up their pre-game show, and the **cadence** of the drums **lulled** me toward sleep.

"I want no mercy on the defense!" Coach shouted, earning some cheers in reply. "I want to keep our offense on the field. And when our offense is on the field, what are we gonna do?"

"Keep 'em guessing!" someone shouted, causing me to blink my eyes open. I yawned again.

"That's right!" Coach cheered. "Now, Riley! Where are you?!"

Everyone turned around to look at me at the exact moment my mouth stretched wide in another tremendous yawn. Silence permeated the room. Coach shot me a look of **tacit** disgust, as if I had just committed the most heinous **effrontery** known to man. Which, I suppose, I had. Here he was, trying to **catalyze** the team for what was sure to be a **combative**, **unrelenting** game, and his captain and quarterback was yawning right in his face.

Abort! *Abort!* My brain cried, long before my lungs took notice.

I snapped my mouth shut. "Right here, coach," I said. My eyes watered from exhaustion.

A bunch of the guys laughed, and Coach narrowed his eyes at me. "We bothering you, Riley?" he asked.

---

cadence: rhythm	**effrontery:** disrespect	**combative:** warlike
lulled: relaxed	**catalyze:** inspire	**unrelenting:** nonstop
tacit: silently expressed		**abort:** end abruptly

"No, Coach," I replied, my face burning.

"Because we can all leave you alone if you need to take a nap," he said, crossing his beefy arms over his chest. More chuckles.

"No, Coach. I'm fine. Sorry," I replied.

"Good. Because today, of all days, I need your head in the game," he said.

"I know, Coach," I replied.

"All right then. Hands in."

A couple of the guys jostled and mocked me as we all huddled up and placed our hands in the center of the circle. Normally I **cherished** these **insular** moments, alone with the team, getting ready for battle. Today I just wanted to be home. Still, I had to play along. I had to make everyone think I was as psyched up as the rest of them.

"Cardinals on three," Coach said. "Ready? One, two, three—Cardinals!"

We all shouted together, then cheered and clapped as the circle broke up and we headed for the doors. I walked up to Coach on the way out, looking for a way to **expiate** my misdeed. Outside, the guys were already making **ribald** jokes about the Washington High cheerleaders, who were also on their way to the field.

"I'm sorry about that, Coach," I told him. "Just had a hard time sleeping last night."

"You all right, Riley? You look a little **wan**," he told me, clearly concerned.

"Yeah. I'm good, Coach. Ready to play," I told him, even as my exhausted body protested. This was ridiculous. I was a **hardy**, young guy. Couldn't I have a couple sleepless nights and still function?

"Good. Because you know you're the **linchpin** of this offense," he said, slapping my shoulder pad. "If I gotta send Warner out there, we're through."

"I know, Coach."

"All right. Let's get out there and give 'em hell," Coach said.

---

cherished: appreciated **insular:** isolated **expiate:** make amends for

ribald: offensive or course **wan:** sickly **hardy:** healthy

linchpin: one that holds a group together

"You got it," I told him.

I pulled my helmet on over my head and jogged after the team, hoping my adrenaline rush would kick in soon and be enough to sustain me through four quarters.

*   *   *   *   *

A **cacophony** out on the street jolted me awake, and as I lifted my head, an **acute** pain shot right through my skull. Sunlight **accosted** my eyes, and as I tried to blink them free of tears, I looked around in confusion. What day was it? Where was I? Was it morning or afternoon, or . . .

And why the hell had I fallen asleep on my desk?

I tried to lift my arm, but it was **flaccid** and full of pins and needles. My face ached, and when I touched it I realized it had been indented with dozens of tiny little marks from the keyboard. I had actually passed out with my cheek pressed against it. Mike Riley had hit a new low.

The moment I thought this, the realization came over me, and I remembered what I had done. I sat there, staring at my computer screen, which still displayed the PokerParty.com game room. My balance stared back at me, the very sight of it **castigating** me for my idiocy: BALANCE $0.

I closed my eyes as the nausea rode over me. It was Monday morning. That noise out on the street was the sound of garbage trucks coming for pickup. It was a school day, and I had been up half the night, losing hand after hand on my computer. And my non-existent PokerParty.com balance wasn't the worst part. The worst part was that, if I had opened my bank's website, my savings account balance would have read exactly the same way.

I had emptied it out. Somewhere around 2 A.M. I had gone all-in on a straight, thinking there was no way I could lose. Feeling

---

cacophony: harsh noise   accosted: attacked   castigating: punishing
acute: sharp   flaccid: limp

as if I were on the brink of winning it all back, rather than on a **precipice** of disaster. And instead, I had lost it all to a guy from Decatur with a straight flush. Lost all of my hard-earned money. Every last cent.

This was a **colossal** disaster. How could I have let this happen? How had I become this **licentious** being? I had gone from Mr. Clean and Responsible to Mr. **Iniquity** in less than two weeks.

"Mike! Time to get up!"

My mother knocked once and walked into the room, just like she did every other morning. She was already fully dressed and coiffed and had her perky smile on. She looked at my bed in confusion, then her brows knit together when she saw my **disheveled** self sitting at the computer. My heart pounding, I **surreptitiously** clicked the Internet browser closed before she could see.

"Michael? What are you doing?" she asked.

"Nothing," I replied automatically.

Slowly, she approached the computer. Oh, God. She *had* seen. She knew what I had done. Okay, this was it. What was I going to do?

Disavow *everything*, a little voice inside me cried. *Plead innocent on all charges.*

I gave her my most **ingenuous** look as she took in the soda cans, empty bag of chips, and whirring computer.

"Michael, were you up all night studying?" she asked, running her hand over my matted hair.

Oh, thank goodness. She thought I was being responsible— which somehow only made me feel even worse than I already did.

"Sweetie, you know I'm all for hard work, but I can't **condone** you sleeping at your desk," she said lightly, planting a kiss on top of my head.

"Sorry, Mom," I said, faking **somnolence** and yawning. In actuality, my pulse was pounding fast enough to keep me awake for days. "I guess I just lost track of time."

---

precipice: cliff
colossal: huge
licentious: immoral
iniquity: wickedness

disheveled: in disarray
surreptitiously: stealthily
disavow: refuse to
acknowledge

ingenuous: honorable
condone: excuse
somnolence: sleepiness

She smiled and cupped my face with her hand. Looking into her **earnest** eyes, I actually felt like crying. She loved me so much and thought I was such a good kid. Little did she know the irresponsible, **wretched** jerk I had become.

"Hop in the shower," she said. "I'll make you breakfast."

There was nothing I could do but **accede**. Go on like it was a normal morning, like my entire world was *not* falling apart. As she shuffled off toward the kitchen, I got up and went about pretending to be the old Mike Riley.

*   *   *   *   *

But the old Mike Riley was officially gone. As I walked into school I was reminded that even my peers were aware that I had changed. The halls before first period were **desolate**, lifeless. People shot me pitying looks or just avoided my gaze altogether. Monday mornings were usually full of **acclaim** and **accolades** for me and the rest of the football team, but that morning the students and teachers alike were just wondering where it had all gone wrong.

Yes, to add insult to injury, Washington High had whipped us on Saturday, largely due to my two interceptions, one of which had been run back for a touchdown. It had been a **grievous** mistake—I had totally misread the defense, and it had cost us the game. The fact that **myriad** people were now trying to prop me up just made the whole thing feel worse.

"You'll get 'em next time, Mike," one of the JV players said to me in the hallway.

"We'll **drub** them at states," Mr. Rowe, my math teacher, added, slapping me on the shoulder.

All this commiserating left me **discomfited** and down. What was even more **disconcerting** was that I hadn't thought about the game all morning. I was so obsessed with the way I had screwed myself

---

earnest: serious
wretched: extremely bad
accede: give consent
desolate: barren
acclaim: applause

accolades: positive acknowledgments
grievous: grave
myriad: a great number

drub: trounce
discomfited: embarrassed and perplexed
disconcerting: upsetting

and my family last night, I hadn't even considered the way I had screwed the whole school on Saturday. Now I realized that it probably would have been smart for me to just stay home.

"So, dude! Really ran us into the ground on Saturday, huh?" Lucas said, laughing as he walked by.

I'm sure he expected me to go off on him, but all I could do was sigh in resignation. Forget going home. This **abnegation** was exactly what I needed. I deserved to be punished.

I loped into history class just before the bell rang. Mr. Weeks walked in and pulled a sheaf of papers out of his battered leather briefcase. An **ominous** silence fell over the room. Our quizzes. He had graded our quizzes. Just what I needed.

"All right, everyone, settle down," he called out, even though everyone was already settled. "Now, I have here your pop quizzes from last week, and I have to say I wasn't very pleased with the results. I didn't think my questions were all that **abstruse**, but apparently they were."

This was not good. If people who had actually *done* the reading had fouled up, I was in deep trouble.

"Now I expect that those of you who didn't bother to do your homework last week will take this as a lesson," he said, walking up and down the aisles and handing the papers back. His ancient shoes squeaked and squished, fraying my already fried nerves. "The next pop quiz will be much more **comprehensive**. If you didn't do well on this one, the next will be extremely difficult for you, so spend the time and do the reading."

He placed my quiz face down on my desk and looked at me **reprovingly**. Not a good sign.

"Once you've all had a chance to study your grades, we'll get started talking about America's role in World War II," he said, moving toward his desk. "I'll give you a couple of minutes to go over your work."

---

abnegation: giving up
ominous: foreboding
abstruse: difficult
comprehensive: extensive
reprovingly: with scorn

My hands quaking, I turned the page over slowly and the grade at the top **truncated** my breath. A big, fat, red F stared back at me. My first F ever. And the feeling of cold dread that came over me made me **wistful** for the days when a C was a big **calamity**. There were red marks everywhere. A quick glance over the page told me that I had gotten exactly one answer correct. I knew that the huge size of the F was intended to **impinge** on my psyche, and it totally worked. This was not part of the normal **vicissitudes** of academic performance. This had happened because of the poker game. It wasn't just affecting my bank account, but my entire life. If I didn't do something to turn things around soon, I was going to be **relegated** to the **remedial** class for the rest of my senior year.

I couldn't let this happen. I folded the paper in half and shoved it in my bag. It was time to regain control of my life.

*   *   *   *   *

The second the bell rang, I was out the door. I had spent Mr. Weeks's entire lecture **concocting** a plan, and now that I had one, I wanted to execute it as quickly as possible. It was time to take **corrective** action. It was time to put the old Mike Riley back into play before it was too late.

"Hey, football star!" Winter greeted me, pushing away from the wall by my locker as I breezed by. She stopped me and wrapped her arms around my neck. "What's going on?"

"Hey," I said, giving her a **perfunctory** kiss and **extricating** myself from her grip. I knew I should stop and give her a little attention. After all, she had spent most of Saturday night trying to cheer me up after my **abysmal** game, but I didn't have time just now. "Sorry. I got something I have to do."

"Nice to blow me off!" she **admonished**, calling after me.

"I'll be right back!" I called over my shoulder.

---

truncated: shortened	**relegated:** demoted	**extricating:** freeing
wistful: dreamy	**remedial:** special education	**abysmal:** absolutely
calamity: disaster	**concocting:** creating	wretched
impinge: trespass	**corrective:** counteracting	**admonished:** scolded
vicissitudes: fluctuations	**perfunctory:** quick	

I just hoped Dominic would be where I expected him to be. I jogged down the main corridor and around the corner into the hallway where the junior lockers were housed. Sure enough, there they were. Dominic and Marcy making out against the wall by her locker. Total creatures of habit. I took a deep breath and walked over to them, my fingers automatically curling into fists.

"Hey, guys!" I said loudly by way of **salutation**. They sprang apart and Marcy looked at me, **disconcerted**.

"Mike! Don't make a scene," Marcy said **querulously**. She probably thought I wanted to fight Dominic or something. *So* the last thing on my mind.

"That's not why I'm here," I said. "In fact, I'm sorry to interrupt, but Dom, can I talk to you for a second?"

He looked at me, baffled, as if my talking to him was **tantamount** to a miracle, which I suppose it was. Last week if you had told me I would be seeking out Dominic Thomas, I would have laughed. But now, I had my reasons.

"What's up?" Dom asked, eyeing me with suspicion as we stepped away from Marcy. He noticed my fists and put a little distance between himself and them. I forced myself to relax my fingers.

"Have you heard about our Wednesday night game?" I asked him pleasantly.

"Yeah," he replied. "Why?"

"Well, I was wondering if you wanted to come this week," I told him. "We had a great time last week. I figured you—"

"Yeah, I heard about your great time," he **interjected** with a smirk. "Didn't my friends go home with all your money?"

My temper flared and my hands curled up again, but I couldn't let his **incendiary** comment get to me. I was here for a reason. I had a plan, maybe not the most **ingenious** plan in the world, but a plan nonetheless. And Dominic was an **integral** part. I shoved my hands into my pockets to hide my aggression.

---

salutation: greeting
disconcerted: confused
querulously: grouchily

tantamount: equal
interjected: interrupted
incendiary: inflammatory

ingenious: clever
integral: necessary

"Yeah, well, regardless . . . I think you should come," I said. "High stakes. It's a lot of fun . . ."

"Thanks anyway, dude," he said, turning away from me. "I'm not much of a gambler. Last week was kind of a fluke for me."

Okay, this was not how this was supposed to go. I needed Dominic to come to that game. He was the only guy I was totally sure I could beat. He was the only sure way to get back my money. There was only one thing I could do.

"What's the matter? Afraid I'll school you again?" I asked.

It was so obviously **calculating** that I was sure he would see right through me. But he paused right in the middle of the hall. Apparently Dominic Thomas was not **intractable** in his resistance to gambling. Thank God. Marcy watched us curiously, twiddling her hair around her finger.

"Dude. Don't even go there," he said, looking at me over his shoulder.

"What?" I said with a shrug. "I understand. You're just being **pragmatic**. I admire it, actually," I said, knowing my wise tone would **exacerbate** his irritation. "Hold on to your money. Play it safe. If that's the kind of guy you are, that's the kind of guy you are."

Dominic turned around and shook his head at me. He knew exactly what I was doing, but it was working anyway. And we both knew it. There was no way Dominic was going to stand there with all those people milling around and let me basically call him a wuss. He stepped right up to me and tipped his chin, staring up into my eyes with a cocky expression.

"All right, man. I'll be there. And this time, you'll be the one getting schooled," he said.

Yeah, right, I thought. "Can't wait," I told him.

I waited for him to return to Marcy's welcoming arms before turning around and heading back to my locker. My mind was about a million times more tranquil now that I had put my plan into play.

---

calculating: scheming   **pragmatic:** sensible   **exacerbate:** add to
intractable: unmanageable

Dom was an abysmal poker player. If I could get him to pony up the big bucks, all I'd have to do was win a few hands and everything would be fine. I was on the road to recovery.

Winter was still waiting for me, but I could tell she was **vexed**.

"Hey there!" I said, laying it on thick and wrapping my arms around her as if nothing had happened. I planted a big kiss on her, and she pulled away.

"What's your problem?" she asked.

"What?" I replied with a grin.

"One second you **ostracize** me, and the next you think you can just come over here and I'll fall at your feet?" she demanded. "Maybe your old girlfriend was all puppy dog like that, but you're with *me* now."

"Geez. Freak out a little why don't you?" I said. "Who knew you were so high-maintenance?" I joked.

I was in a good mood, feeling lighter than I had in days, and I expected her to pick up on it—to laugh and joke back. But instead her eyes clouded over.

"Ha ha," she said flatly. "Why don't you give me a call when you get that **discombobulated** head of yours in order?"

Then she turned around and strutted down the hall, leaving me slack-jawed behind her. What on earth had just happened here?

---

vexed: annoyed   **ostracize:** shut out   **discombobulated:** confused

Okay. So I *had* blown Winter off at first, which was not cool. After all, with all the insanity in my life right then, she was the best thing I had going for me. It was total **serendipity** that someone so cool and funny and **vivacious** had come into my life right when everything else was so **odious**. There was no way I wanted to screw up our **nascent** relationship, so I decided to make it up to her. I came up with a perfect plan, and I wanted it to be a surprise. So that day at lunch, I invited her over to study later that night. She looked at me a bit suspiciously when I asked, but agreed.

My parents had a PTA meeting that evening, so Winter and I would have the place to ourselves. She showed up right on time, and when I answered the door, I was nearly stunned by her **pulchritude**. Under her denim jacket, she wore a white sweater with a furry collar, and her cheeks were flushed pink from the chilly autumn air. Every time I saw her, I swear she got more and more gorgeous.

"Hi! Thanks for coming," I said.

"Hey there, football star," she said with a smirk. She shrugged out of her jacket and shoved it at me rather roughly as she passed me by. She stopped at the entryway to the living room, where I had dimmed the lights and lit a bunch of candles. On the table was an overflowing bowl of popcorn, several smaller bowls of candy, and a stack of DVDs.

"So, this is your den of iniquity?" she asked. "I like the snacks. Nice touch."

"Huh?" I looked over my shoulder as I hung up her jacket in the front closet. It smelled like strawberry gum. "My what of what?" I asked.

---

serendipity: good luck   **odious:** hateful   **pulchritude:** beauty
vivacious: lively   **nascent:** new

"Don't forget who you're dealing with here," Winter said, dropping down on the couch. "I know your parents are both teachers, and I know they're out tonight. Why do I know this? Because my mom is on the PTA. And I know how you guys and your **prurient** minds work. So when you invited me over here to 'study,'" she said, throwing in some air quotes, "on the one night your house is deserted, I knew you had only one thing on your mind."

She looked at me with a teasing, knowing smile. I stared at her from the doorway. "Your mind works in mysterious ways," I said.

"Please! Don't try to deny it. What are these, porn?" she said, grabbing the first movie off the stack. She looked at the title and her jaw dropped slightly. Now it was my turn to smirk. "*Fools Rush In?*" she read, then picked up the next movie. "*While You Were Sleeping . . . Just Married . . . You've Got Mail . . . 13 Going on 30*. Oh my God. It's the most **vacuous** collection of films I've ever seen. Where did you get all these?"

"From my mom's collection," I said, sitting down next to her. "She watches them **incessantly**. She loves them too, although for very different reasons than you."

"I don't believe you did this," Winter said, looking around at all my efforts, **enthralled**. Clearly she was seeing the room in a whole new way. "I'm so sorry. When you said you wanted to study, I figured it was a **spurious** story—"

"Well it was, just not for the **deviant** reasons you had in mind. This was just a surprise to apologize for being such a moron this morning," I said. Then I slid a bit closer to her and wrapped my arms around her tiny frame. "Although, you did come over even though you thought I was going to try something, so if you *were* interested . . . ," I joked, waggling my eyebrows.

She whacked my arm. "Hey. Don't make me repent my **repentance**," she said.

prurient: lewd	**incessantly:** constantly	**deviant:** twisted
vacuous: unintelligent	**enthralled:** captivated	**repentance:** regret
	spurious: bogus	

"All right. Can't blame me for trying," I said, pulling away with my hands raised. She rolled her eyes at me. "But seriously, I just wanted to apologize for blowing you off by the lockers," I told her. "I had a lot on my mind, but it's no excuse."

"Darn tootin'" she said.

"Did you just say 'darn tootin'?" I asked.

"I'm a very layered and complex person," she replied, grabbing a handful of popcorn.

"Also big on **extolling** your own virtues, I notice," I teased. She tossed half the popcorn in my face, and it tumbled down my shirt. Point taken. "All right then. Which should we watch first?" I asked, brushing myself clean.

"First? We can't watch all of these. We'll be here all night," Winter protested. "And in case you're forgetting, it *is* Monday."

"I know. But I was thinking we could make it sort of a standing date," I told her. "Every week we can watch another one, and you can tell me how **rife** each one is with problems."

I knew that this plan implied that I was hoping for a long-term relationship here, and I wondered how she would take it. She didn't even seem to notice. I wasn't sure if that was a good sign or a bad sign, but I would have to roll with it.

"Ooh! I like it," Winter said, bright-eyed. "Then let's start with *13 Going on 30*. The laughable scenes are **manifold**. Plus they acted like it was all high-concept, but it is *so* **derivative** of like a million movies. I really felt bad for Mark Ruffalo, I gotta say. But then he went and made *Just Like Heaven*, which kind of made me wonder about his intelligence."

"Wow. You've really put a lot of thought into this," I said, popping the movie in.

Winter smiled. "You have no idea."

We settled back into the couch together to watch, and as Winter curled into my side, I realized I hadn't felt so **serene** in days. Just

---

extolling: raving about **manifold:** abundant **serene:** calm
rife: overflowing **derivative:** copied

having her with me calmed all my tensions and guilt and fear. For the next two hours, I resolved that I wasn't going to think about gambling or my mistakes. I was only going to think about her.

"This is really cool, Mike. I wish I could do something to **reciprocate**," she said as the movie started. Then she turned her face toward mine and kissed me.

I smiled happily. "That's all you needed to do."

*   *   *   *   *

The night of the high-stakes game, I was feeling a bit **timorous** as I approached the basement door to Ian's house. What I was about to do was not going to be easy, but I couldn't see any other way out. I just hoped that Ian would be **amenable** to my plan. After all, the whole thing hinged on him.

I took a deep breath and walked in. The stereo was on at a high volume, and Ian was puttering around, setting up the tables. He looked up when I closed the door. I was about half an hour early, but Ian looked **inordinately** surprised at my arrival. Didn't I usually show up before everyone else?

"Hey, man," he said. "What're you doing here?"

All the blood in my body instantly rushed to my face. Was he **insinuating** that I didn't belong here? This game was my idea. "What do you mean?" I said **indignantly**. "I came to play."

Ian blinked, nonplussed. "Oh . . . okay," he said, pushing in a chair.

"What?" I asked. I had never felt so unwelcome in my best friend's house. In fact, I felt **conspicuously** out of place.

He walked by me and turned the stereo off. For a few seconds he stood there with his back to me, and my body temperature slowly crept higher and higher. What was going on here? What was he thinking?

---

reciprocate: exchange in kind
timorous: timid

amenable: agreeable
inordinately: unusually
insinuating: suggesting

indignantly: angrily
conspicuously: distinctly

"It's just . . ." He finally turned around, but it seemed like he was having trouble looking me in the eye. "After last week's games I wasn't sure if you were exactly . . . uh . . . **solvent**," he said finally.

He looked extremely uncomfortable as he said this, and I felt a rush of humiliation and anger. Had he been feeling sorry for me all week? Was I that deserving of his pity?

"I mean, correct me if I'm wrong, but you kind of lost a lot of money on Wednesday," he said. "And then again on Friday . . ."

I don't know why this irritated me so much. It was, after all, true. And besides, the fact that he realized this made the conversation we were about to have a lot easier. I wasn't going to have to explain every awful detail of what I had done and then endure his shock.

I took another deep breath and told myself to chill. "Actually, that's kinda what I wanted to talk to you about."

"What's that?" Ian asked warily.

"Well, I've gotten myself into kind of a mess," I said, the shame almost overwhelming. I sat down on one of the leather couches in the corner and found it easier to hang my head than to look at my best friend. "I'm not **inextricably** in trouble or anything," I added quickly. "But I might need your help."

"You want to borrow money," Ian said flatly. His tone was totally dead, as if I was asking him for a kidney transplant or something.

"Just a little," I said quickly. "Nothing **exorbitant**." At least it wouldn't be for him. The kid was rolling in cash even *without* his weekly percentage from the games.

"It's not like you can buy into this game with a **pittance**," Ian said. As if I didn't know that. Since when did he **condescend** to me?

"I *know* that, E," I shot back, looking at him for the first time. "Why are you being such a bastard about this?"

His eyes flashed, and I realized the **temerity** of my outburst. Good friends or not, it probably wasn't a good idea to insult the person you were asking a favor of.

---

solvent: financially sound   **exorbitant:** excessive   **condescend:** talk down
inextricably: inescapably   **pittance:** little bit   **temerity:** boldness

"Look, I just need to get into this game. Dominic's coming, and we already know the kid sucks. Plus, he and his stupid friends *love* to throw their money around. I know I can beat these guys," I told him firmly. "I *know* I can."

"Very **quixotic** of you, Mike," he said. "But I think you proved last week that poker isn't *just* about skill."

"Dude, what's your problem?" I said.

"Nothing! It's just, I'm worried about you, man," Ian said. "You seem a little desperate, and I'm not totally sure this is a **scrupulous** plan."

I stood up, adrenaline pumping through my veins. "What the hell, E? I thought we were friends. Now it's like you're questioning my **probity**." I wasn't usually one to **emote** like this, but lately my feelings were so all over the place I couldn't keep them in **check**.

"No!" Ian said. "No, I'm not. It's just . . . I'm worried about you, man."

I knew he was just trying to be a good friend, but somehow this was the most humiliating **utterance** I'd heard yet. "Well, thanks, but I don't need you to be worried about me. I need you to help me." At that moment, I'll admit it, I was desperate.

He rubbed his hands over his face, and I knew I was making him uncomfortable. I almost felt bad for putting him in a difficult spot, but this wasn't a **rash** decision, it was my only choice. If Ian **forsook** me, there was absolutely no way out. I was going to have to go to my parents and tell them what I had done. I was going to have to deal with the very real consequences of throwing away my life's savings, whatever they turned out to be.

"Come on, man. Please," I said, knowing I was being **pertinacious**. "Just help me out this one time."

Ian looked at me, and I could tell he was weighing his options. I begged him silently. If I couldn't count on my friends, who could I count on? I couldn't even imagine the depth of the pit I was going to

quixotic: bold	**emote**: express emotion	**rash**: careless
scrupulous: careful	**check**: restraint	**forsook**: abandoned
probity: honor	**utterance**: pronouncement	**pertinacious**: headstrong

fall into if he said no.

"Okay, fine," he said finally with a sigh. "I'll buy you in, but that's it."

I was so relieved I could have collapsed, but instead I gave him a quick hug. My gratitude was that **ineffable**.

"Thanks, man."

"Yeah," he said with a smile. "You better be **indefatigable** tonight."

I grinned back. "That's my plan," I said.

It was, in fact, the only option. If I didn't win, I was screwed.

* * * * *

I didn't win. Dominic and his friends came to play, and I must have been distracted by my desperation, because they **razed** me. I didn't pick up on any of their **semaphores**, and, in fact, I misread quite a few. The more money I lost, the more hampered my instincts became. On one hand, I got Dominic's tells mixed up with Lucas's, and I ended up betting the farm on crappy cards, thinking Dom was bluffing. It turned out he had four of a kind, and he collected all my cash, to the **plaudits** of his friends and lackeys who had turned out in droves.

"You ready to surrender yet, Mikey?" Dominic asked, laughing. He had been **inimical** toward me all night. Not that I was surprised. I *had* manipulated him into coming here. I suppose, on some level, I deserved his **noxious** behavior. It was amazing how much less combative I felt toward him now that I had a girlfriend whom I really liked. His taking Marcy from me no longer seemed like such a big deal. Taking my money, however, was huge.

I glanced at Ian. Dom and his friends had **pillaged** the cash he had lent me. Now it was either borrow more or go home with my tail between my legs. That feeling of helplessness is **indescribable**.

---

ineffable: beyond words
indefatigable: untiring
razed: flattened
semaphores: signals

plaudits: cheers
inimical: antagonistic
noxious: poisonous

pillaged: looted
indescribable: beyond description

Only people who have played and lost at poker know how horrible it is. Luckily, Ian was one of those people. He got up and took out a few more stacks of chips. I shot him a grateful look as he handed them over. My best friend had a **surfeit** of kindness. Or maybe it was just his pride talking on my behalf. Maybe he just wanted me to beat these suckers as much as I wanted to beat them.

"You're staying in?" Dominic said mirthfully. "Great! After tonight I'm gonna be able to put that new sound system in the Bimmer."

You would think that hundreds of games of poker with my friends would have **inured** me to the trash-talking, but coming from this guy it got under my skin.

Ian, who was standing behind me, leaned toward my ear. "Will you take this **haughty** asshole down already?"

I smiled. "Will do."

But my confidence was **evanescent** and, ultimately, **ineffectual**. On the next few hands it wasn't just Dominic who schooled me, it was all the **tangential** players as well. My money slowly **dissipated** around the table, filling each of their pockets. I just could not get the cards. There seemed to be a **plenitude** of threes and fours in the deck and not a single royal. At least not for me. It got to the point where I was actually trying to sneak a peak at everyone else's cards, but as dull as these guys were, they were at least smart enough to **obscure** their hole cards from view.

Finally, *finally*, I was dealt a good hand. Between my hole cards and the cards on the table I had four jacks. Four of a kind in royals is really solid. The most solid hand I had had all night. If I wasn't going to win on this one, I wasn't going to win on anything. Every time someone rose, I called. The pot grew huge, and I started to salivate, even as my heart pounded with trepidation.

I looked at Ian before he dealt the river. I could tell he was just as nervous as I was. I didn't even want to think about what would

---

surfeit: excess
inured: accustomed
haughty: arrogant
evanescent: fleeting
ineffectual: worthless
tangential: peripheral
dissipated: scattered
plenitude: abundance
obscure: hide

happen if I lost this hand. Not only would I be broke, but I would also be in debt to my best friend—a debt I had no possible way of paying back. Why had I not thought of all this before?

I guess I hadn't *wanted* to think about it.

"Dealing the river," Ian announced.

The card was useless to me. I already had my hand. He dealt a queen, and I looked around at the remaining players. I couldn't read any of their reactions for all the money in the world. My **perspicacity** was out the window.

"I'm in," Lucas said.

"I call," John added, throwing in his chips.

"Me too," Dominic said, adding his own.

I pushed my own chips in.

"Well? Whadaya got?" I demanded.

"Three of a kind," Lucas said, tossing his cards down. He had three queens and was a looking a little too confident about it, if you asked me.

"Got me beat," John said, throwing out his cards face down.

Yes! That left only Dominic. Only his cards could **inhibit** me from winning the pot. I did the math in my mind. If I won this hand, I could pay back both Ian's loans and still have some money to keep me alive.

Please just don't let him have the cards, I thought. *I need this. I need this more than anything in the world.*

"Riley?" he said, raising his eyebrows.

I swallowed hard. My hands shaking, I laid my cards down. "Four of a kind," I said, trying not to let my terror show.

Dominic sighed hugely. My outlook brightened. I had him! I had him, I had him, I had him!

Slowly he leaned forward and placed his cards down. I stared at them for a moment, as did everyone else. Silence fell as we all tried to work out what he had.

---

perspicacity: insight   **inhibit:** prevent

"Oh, sorry," Dominic said. "That would be a straight flush. Did I not say that?"

"Oh!" his friends cheered, slapping hands and laughing. Laughing at my expense.

I felt like I was going to throw up. I leaned back in my chair as my life flashed before my eyes, my many transgressions of the past couple of weeks acting as highlights. And they just kept celebrating. Celebrating my misery.

"What do you think, Riley?" Dominic asked. "Want to borrow some more cash and go again?"

I glared at him, seething. Did I say I was feeling less combative toward this guy? I lied. I wanted to hit him so badly my fingers itched. I wanted to tackle him to the ground and wipe that **recalcitrant** smirk right off his pointy little face. I started to get up to do just that, but Ian jumped right out of his chair.

"All right, guys. Game's over!" he announced. "Let's get everybody cashed out."

"What? Tired of bankrolling your little friend?" Dominic asked.

Ian placed a firm hand on my shoulder to keep me from lunging at the guy. "It's getting late, and this is my house," he told the guys firmly. "It's time to go."

All I could do was sit there and stew as Ian handed over all that cash and Dom and his friends all sashayed out, their wallets full to bursting. Four guys who definitely didn't need the money. Four guys who would never have to worry about working a part-time job or paying for college.

I hated them. I hated them all. But most of all, I hated myself.

*   *   *   *   *

I moved over to the couch as Ian saw the guys out. Sometimes, when he thinks we're going to be too rowdy or **strident**, he walks

---

recalcitrant: disobedient   strident: loud

us to our cars to make sure we keep it down. I had a feeling that tonight it was less about keeping the game a secret from his parents than it was about giving me some time to collect myself. I was grateful for it.

As I sat there, my head hanging, I felt nauseated and trapped. My last **vestige** of hope was gone. I was dead. I was totally dead. There was no way I could keep my **turpitude** from my parents anymore. For the past week, every day I got home and checked the mail for the bank statements, my heart in my throat until I went through every last envelope. So far, I had been lucky, but it had to be coming any day now. And when it did, my parents would know everything.

The door to the basement opened, and I sat up straight. First things first. I had to make things right with Ian.

"Dude, I am so sorry," I said. "I know where I can get the money to pay you back," I lied. If I knew where I could get money, I'd be getting it for myself so I could **reconcile** my savings account.

"It's okay," Ian said. He seemed tired. Tired and disappointed. "Don't worry about it."

"No. That's not an option," I told him, standing. "I'm going to pay you back."

"Oh, I know," he replied. "I just meant you shouldn't be sorry. I wouldn't have lent you the money if I hadn't wanted to."

For a moment I just stood there. I felt as if he had slapped me across the face. For that split second I thought he had meant he would eat the loan, and the moment I realized he *hadn't* meant that, I felt betrayed. But still, he was right. I borrowed money from him, and I should pay it back.

"Oh. Okay. Good," I said.

"But listen," he said, shifting his weight from foot to foot. "I think you need to take a little **hiatus** from these games. In fact, I think you shouldn't play again until you've paid me back."

---

vestige: sign   **reconcile:** settle   **hiatus:** break
turpitude: corruption

He looked me in the eye, and my mouth suddenly felt **desiccated**. Was he seriously issuing a **mandate** here? To me? His best friend? Forget the fact that I was, at this point, basically **indigent**—that I wouldn't have had the money to play even if I wanted to. But who was he to tell me what I could and couldn't do?

"I'm sorry, are you *forbidding* me from playing poker?" I snapped. "I said I was going to pay you back."

"It's not about the money," Ian said. "It's you. I'm worried about you."

"Oh, here we go again," I said **scathingly**, throwing my hands up. "Since when is it your job to protect me?"

"Someone's gotta do it!" he replied. "You haven't exactly been exercising **temperance** around here lately. You've been **hemorrhaging** money, and it's like you don't even know how to stop."

"Hey! You're the one who gave me that second loan," I told him.

"And you're the one who lost it!" he shouted.

"Oh, that's great. So this *is* about the money," I said. "You decide I'm a **liability**, so I'm out. These are your **punitive** measures?"

"You are so **solipsistic**," he spat at me. "Like *I'm* the one who's doing something to *you*. You're the one who keeps betting even though you have no money. You're my best friend. I don't want to see you get into more trouble."

"And you're so wise all of a sudden," I said. "You know exactly how to help me."

"It's not like that," he **railed**.

"You know, if you hadn't started up those Friday night games in the first place, I wouldn't be in this mess," I told him.

Ian's eyes went wide. "So, what? You're going to blame all this on me?"

Why not? It was the only way I could think of to **exonerate** myself. And I needed to free myself from blame. I didn't think I could live with this crushing guilt one second longer.

---

desiccated: dried up	**temperance:** self-restraint	**solipsistic:** self-centered
mandate: order	**hemorrhaging:** bleeding	**railed:** protested
indigent: poor	**liability:** burden	**exonerate:** clear
scathingly: cruelly	**punitive:** disciplinary	

"Hey. Just calling 'em like I see 'em," I said, knowing my argument was **tenuous** at best.

Ian shook his head. His expression was almost disgusted, which made me feel like the mud caked on the bottom of my shoe. "I can't believe you're so **perfidious**. We've always had a good time at these games. *You're* the one who begged me to start up another one. It's not my fault if you can't control yourself, Mike."

His comment stung. I couldn't believe he called *me* disloyal, then said something like that. If anyone was a bad friend around here, it was him.

"Thanks a lot." My skin flushed hot, and I grabbed my jacket. "I'm outta here."

He didn't even try to stop me as I stormed out the door.

tenuous: weak   perfidious: two-faced

Chapter Eight

That Friday night we had a game under the lights on our home field, an occasion everyone at school **salivated** for. There was nothing like the **atmosphere** at a night game. The stands were packed with **revelers**, bundled up against the cold, **bedecked** in our school colors of red and black. The stadium was **effulgent** with the glow of hundreds of floodlights. As we raced out onto the field in a pack, jumping and shouting and cheering, the energy in the air was **palpable**. And unlike last week's game, this time I couldn't wait to get out on the field and kick a little ass. The insanity in the air perfectly **complemented** my own. I felt as if I were about to explode from the **multifarious** emotions that had been warring for my attention all week long. At turns I felt guilty, scared, sad, and disappointed, but most of all, angry. Angry with Ian for being such a jerk on Wednesday, yeah, but mostly angry with myself. That anger had been building up, day by day, to the point where I was going to have to take it out on someone or something. I pitied the guy who took the brunt of my **kinetic** energy.

We were playing the Westmont Bears, a team that was in our league but had never beaten us in the last four years. Normally we viewed this game as a gimme, but this season they were undefeated—**indomitable**—largely due to a wicked defense led by the **stellar** performance of their right nose tackle, Tony Odewale. He was a senior and was well on his way to a season record for sacks. He was going to be my primary **antagonist** tonight.

Bring it on, I thought, looking for him on the visitor's sidelines as we gathered on our own side. The Westmont cheerleaders danced around in their **garish** silver and gold uniforms, blocking the team

---

salivated: drooled
atmosphere: mood
revelers: celebrators
bedecked: dressed
effulgent: shining

palpable: noticeable, touchable
complemented: completed
multifarious: intricate
kinetic: related to motion or force

indomitable: steadfast
stellar: outstanding
antagonist: enemy
garish: gaudy

from view. But I knew Odewale was there somewhere, lusting for my blood, just like I was lusting for his. Anyone's. My own would have probably **sufficed** at this point.

As we waited for the kickoff, I blew into my **chapped** hands, my breath making clouds in the **arid** air. I bounced up and down on the balls of my feet, primed for **conflict**. Behind me, the crowd started up a chant, and I turned around to scan the bleachers. I found Winter and her friends almost instantly and lifted a hand. She smiled and waved back. Her Goth troop held up a sign that said "Rip 'Em to Pieces." I think this was the first game they had ever actually sat down for. But then, there was always an **eclectic** mix of people at Friday night games—many of whom never bothered to show up for Saturday games but came Friday night just for the social aspects.

One person who was not there, however, was my buddy Ian. No. He was back home hosting his regular Friday night game. A game that I would have been at, winning my money back, if not for this schedule conflict. And, oh yeah, if Ian hadn't **banned** me from the **premises**.

Oh yeah. I was ready to beat someone down.

The ball was kicked off, and it seemed to hang in the air forever before Donnie Henderson, our kick-return specialist, finally caught it. He **executed** some sick moves, spinning out of one tackle and jumping over another guy who was going for his ankles before **accelerating** up field. Donnie was one of the more **agile** guys on the team, and he was thrilling to watch. The entire crowd went nuts as he made it out to the 48-yard line before getting slammed by a humongous defender.

"All right, team, let's **expunge** these guys!" Coach shouted.

We cheered and slapped each other's backs as we took the field. My heart pounded like crazy as we lined up behind the ball. There was Odewale, staring me down from the other side.

---

sufficed: been enough
chapped: rough
arid: dry
conflict: battle

eclectic: varied
banned: barred
premises: property
executed: carried out

accelerating: speeding up
agile: nimble
expunge: destroy

"I'm coming for you, Riley," he growled, sounding **feral** and more than a little bit scary. A dark eye shield and blood-red mouth guard **accentuated** his threatening appearance. "You're gonna be eating dirt in about five seconds."

I ignored him. The **braggart** had no idea the amount of adrenaline I was working on tonight. He thought he was freaking me out? Hardly. A little **adversity** was exactly what I needed.

"Blue thirty-two! Blue thirty-two!" I shouted, looking up and down the line, checking the **configuration** of the defense. Looked like they were double-teaming Daryl, our number-one receiver. No matter. I had other options.

"Hike!" I shouted.

I dropped back to pass. My center and one of the guards took on Odewale, acting as a **buffer** for me. I scanned the field, but none of the receivers were open. I had about two seconds to make the play.

Oh, crap! Make that half a second. Odewale tossed Morris Johnson aside with serious **brutality**—and Morris weighs almost three hundred pounds—then ducked and let the guard fall right over him. **Unencumbered** now, he raced right at me, unbelievably fast for a guy his size. Watching him bear down on me was like watching a charging elephant coming my way. I tucked the ball and dodged. His helmet glanced off my thigh pad as he dove for me. For a split second he had hold of my foot, but I evaded him. I dodged another defender and ran right, taking a **circuitous** route toward the sideline around the battling linemen. Still no one was open downfield, and I was almost over the line of scrimmage.

There was nothing left to do now but run.

As I raced down the field, I pointed out a defender to one of my linemen, begging for the block. Rob Moore slammed into the guy, and I dodged their falling bodies. As I ran, I could *feel* the defenders breathing down my neck, and I turned it on. *Screw these guys. Screw Ian. Screw Dominic and his stupid friends. Screw the bank*

---

feral: wild
accentuated: accented
braggart: boaster

adversity: hardship
configuration: setup
buffer: cushion

brutality: savagery
unencumbered: burden-free
circuitous: roundabout

and the poker website and my own stupid guilt. I ran as fast as I could, and each passing yard **mitigated** my pent-up frustrations a bit more. I could hear the crowd screaming and the **amplified** voice of the announcer marking my progress.

"Riley to the fifteen. To the ten! He's got one man to beat! Riley to the five and . . . *TOUCHDOWN!*"

I spiked the ball in the end zone, hard, expelling even more of my wild emotions. My team rushed me, and we slammed chests and hugged. The feeling was **comparable** to nothing. I had scored a rushing touchdown on the first play from scrimmage. I could still do some things right.

I turned toward the crowd and leapt up and down, my fists in the air, egging them on. For the first time all week, I felt sheer joy and I wanted to hold on to it, **immerse** myself in it, wrap it all around me and never let it go. These Westmont kids had no idea what they were in for. Tonight I was going to be a one-man wrecking machine.

*   *   *   *   *

"And that's the end of the game! The Hillside Cardinals beat the Westmont Bears, forty-two to seven!" the announcer cried. "Let's hear it for Mike Riley and the entire Cardinals team!"

The crowd went crazy, **exalting** us with cheers and rushing the field. I was crowded by hundreds of people, adults and kids, guys and girls, everyone **according** their **adulation** to me. I took it all in, **ecstatic** over the win. We had just run all over the most dominant defense in the league. This was a huge triumph. If someone had told me yesterday that the score would be forty-two to seven in our favor, that Odewale would not have recorded a single sack, I would never have thought it **conceivable**.

"Hey, Mike! Mike Riley!" a slightly older guy cried, waving a

---

mitigated: diminished
amplified: boosted
comparable: equivalent

immerse: sink
exalting: applauding
according: giving

adulation: praise
ecstatic: overjoyed
conceivable: imaginable

tape-recorder at me as he tried to navigate the crowd. "I'm Seth Meisel from the *Hillside Gazette*! Can I get a quote?"

"Guys! Guys! Let him through!" I said, dispersing the fans who **fettered** the reporter. He shot me a thankful smile as he finally broke through the masses and hit the record button on his recorder.

"Hey, man," I said as people screamed and cheered all around me.

"So, Mike Riley, how does it feel to be the **paragon** of New York state football?" he asked, shoving the little microphone at me.

I laughed, for some reason, as the guilt started to creep back over my shoulders. "I don't feel like a paragon of anything," I told him. "It was a team effort tonight, and I'm just really proud of my guys."

"And he's even modest," Seth said, amused. "The **consensus** in the stands and at the paper is that you'll be going to a top-ten school next year. Division One. What do you think about that?"

"I think it'd be great," I said. "But right now I just want to concentrate on a winning season for the Cardinals."

The team started to head for the locker room, and I made to follow. "Thanks, man. I gotta go."

"Thanks, Mike! Good luck with the rest of the season!" he called after me.

On the way toward the school, I tried to keep the smile plastered to my face, but already the feeling of victory was waning. I could hear the guys' cheers echoing off the locker room walls up ahead and wished I could **bypass** the usual post-win celebration and the coach's **laudatory** remarks, but I knew I had no choice. If I skipped out, it would mean *days* of explaining to my teammates, and I wouldn't even have a **plausible** excuse. I just had to try to stay **composed** and get through it.

Inside, everyone cheered my arrival and slapped my shoulder pads and back. I smiled genuinely as Daryl ruffled my sweaty hair and someone popped a fizzed-up Sprite, spraying it all over the room

---

fettered: restrained   **bypass:** avoid   **plausible:** believable
paragon: perfect example   **laudatory:** praising   **composed:** calm
consensus: agreement

like champagne. Finally Coach came in and settled everyone down. As much as they could be settled, anyway.

"Well guys, I think you silenced any **detractors** you had after last week's loss," he began.

"Yeah!" everyone shouted, slapping hands and getting riled up all over again. Coach waited for us to quiet down, grinning all the while.

"You guys played sixty minutes of perfect football out there tonight, and I'm proud of you," he said to the tune of more cheers. He picked up the game ball from behind him and held it up. "But I think we all know who's going home with this."

"Mikey!" one of the linemen shouted, earning laughter and more cheers.

"Mike Riley, get up here!" Coach said.

I contemplated bolting. I wasn't feeling all that **meritorious** at the moment, but my teammates basically shoved me out of my seat and up to the front of the room.

"Mike, you passed for two-hundred thirteen yards, three touchdowns, and one rushing touchdown," Coach said. "I think we can all agree that you are the **incontrovertible** MVP of this game. Congratulations."

My teammates gave me a standing **ovation** as I humbly accepted the game ball. I tried to take my seat, but Coach clasped my shoulder pad in his strong grip and kept me where I was.

"All right, all of you. Get out there and celebrate!" Coach shouted. "Safely, of course," he added. Then he turned to me and lowered his voice. "You. Come with me."

Confused, I followed Coach to his office. He let me in first, then he closed the door behind him.

"Son, that was one of the most unbelievable performances I have ever seen at a high school level," he said with a grin as he stepped behind his desk. "If you keep playing like that, schools are going to be throwing scholarship money at you."

---

detractors: naysayers
meritorious: worthy of honor

incontrovertible: indisputable

ovation: round of clapping

I swallowed hard. Money. It was all about money. Too bad I couldn't have them throwing cash at me right now instead of at the end of the year. That would have solved all of my problems.

"Tomorrow I am going to spend my day making phone calls, inviting scouts to come out and **appraise** your performance next week," he told me. "It's the big rivalry game against Dorchester, and we both know it's gonna be out of control. You go out there and do what you did tonight, it's going to be seriously **advantageous** to your **prospects**."

He took a deep breath and looked at me wistfully. "You're going places, kid."

I nodded. "Thanks, Coach."

Somehow the images of my bright future, **juxtaposed** against the images of my awful present, were just bringing me down more.

He blinked, clearly **bewildered**. "What's the matter? You think this is all a **fabrication**? Some fairy tale I concocted to amuse you? I'm telling you, you're going to get a scholarship to a top school. I'm thinking about the NFL draft in a few years. This is no time to **conserve** your energy, kid. You're allowed to get a little excited."

"I know, Coach," I said, quickly. "Sorry, I'm just . . . I guess I'm coming down a little."

"Well, that much is **patent**," he said. "But don't let yourself. This was a huge game, kid. Get out there and enjoy it with the men."

He came around his desk and put his hand on my shoulder. "And I know you're generally a modest kid, but tonight you could probably even **boast** a little and no one would hold it against you."

I smirked and nodded again. "Thanks, Coach. Really."

"Thank *you*, son," he said.

He opened the door and slapped me on the back, pushing me toward the locker room. As soon as the door was closed behind me, I turned and walked the other way, leaving the joyous sounds of my team and their cheers behind.

---

appraise: judge
advantageous: favorable
prospects: future opportunities

juxtaposed: contrasted
bewildered: confused
fabrication: lie

conserve: save
patent: apparent
boast: brag

* * * * *

I arrived at my dark, empty house, still clad in my grass- and dirt-stained uniform. My parents were out with friends for the evening, which was good because I didn't feel like relating all the triumphs of the game to them just now. I walked into the kitchen, flicked on the light, and froze in my tracks. The mail was there, sitting on the corner of the table, and right on top was the monthly bank statement.

It was amazing how something that was once so **benign** could now be the **bane** of my existence. I first felt a **compulsion** to grab it, tear it up, and bury the pieces all over the backyard, but I knew that wouldn't help my situation. Instead I picked up the envelope and, pulse racing through my ears, brought it back to my room. At the very least, I could get it out of plain sight for now. Maybe I could buy myself some time.

I sat down on the edge of my bed with the envelope in my lap and stared at it. Right then, all my teammates were out somewhere **carousing** and celebrating our victory. I was sitting alone in my room with a bank statement. Could my life get any more depressing?

I thought about opening the envelope, but I couldn't. I knew what it would say, but the very idea of those zeros staring back at me made me sick. Instead I picked up the phone and dialed Winter's cell.

"Hey, football star! Where are you?! The whole world wants to **douse** you in Gatorade!" she shouted, with much noise in the background. "Not that I would let them," she added slyly.

"Can you come over?" I blurted.

"What's wrong?" she asked, her tone changing immediately to one of concern.

"I just . . . I need to talk to you," I said, squeezing my eyes closed.

"I'll be right there," she assured me. Then the line went dead.

I tossed the phone on the bed, shoved the bank statement under my pillow to get it out of my sight, and headed for the shower. Winter

---

benign: harmless
bane: burden
compulsion: need
carousing: frolicking
douse: soak

would know what to do. She would be able to come up with a plan. And even if she couldn't, just her presence would be a temporary **antidote** for my distress.

*　*　*　*　*

I was still wet from the shower when Winter showed up.

"Hey," she said cautiously. "Are you all right?"

"Not really," I replied. "I need to talk to you. Thanks for coming."

"No problem," she said, my comments clearly **augmenting** her concern.

I brought her back to my room and sat her down on the bed. I had no idea whether she was going to offer **condemnation** or **consolation**, but I was hoping for the latter. Of course, once she was there, I had trouble finding the words. I took a step back and started to pace. How was I going to tell her this? She knew about the first game but had no clue how deep a hole I had dug for myself since then. What if she just **berated** me and stormed out? At this point, it was probably the reaction I deserved.

"Mike, can you just tell me what's going on?" she asked finally. "'Cuz you're starting to freak me out here."

"Sorry. Okay," I said. I took a deep breath and looked her in the eye. "I'm kind of in a lot of trouble."

Winter leaned forward as I told her the whole story. Once I got started I became quite **garrulous**, actually. I told her all about the high-stakes game and Dominic and his friends and how I had thought they were so easy to beat. While I spoke, she listened carefully, **commiserating** at all the right moments and growing paler and paler as I related the amounts of money I had lost.

"So . . . what's the **cumulative** damage?" she asked finally. "How much have you actually lost?"

---

antidote: cure
augmenting: adding to
condemnation: blame

consolation: comfort
berated: criticized, chewed out
garrulous: talkative

commiserating: sympathizing
cumulative: total

I swallowed against a dry throat. "All of it," I said. "Every last dime."

Winter whistled long and low. She leaned back on her hands. "Well. That *is* quite the **quandary**," she said.

"Tell me about it," I replied, sitting down next to her. I put my head in my hands and stared at the floor. At least she wasn't flipping out. Her calm **demeanor** seemed like a **propitious** sign.

"Sorry," I said. "When I asked you out, you probably thought you were getting involved with this upstanding, responsible guy. I feel like I misled you," I added with a wry laugh.

Winter leaned over and kissed me on the cheek. "It's cool. It actually kind of makes you more interesting," she joked. And I laughed. Even in all my misery, I laughed.

"So, forgive me if I'm suggesting the obvious here, but why don't you just get a job?" she asked.

"I would, but I have a deal with my parents," I told her. "I'm only allowed to have part-time jobs during the summer and when it's not football season. They want any time I'm not spending on practice and games to be spent studying. They're afraid that if I try to do too much my grades will suffer."

The **irony**, of course, was that they were suffering anyway.

"So if you got a job now, they would be suspicious," she said.

"They would probably make me quit," I replied with a nod.

Winter took a deep breath and blew it out. She stood up and ran her hands through her hair, contemplating me. As she bit her lip, I knew she was forming a plan. I just had no idea what it might be.

"What's up?" I asked.

"Well, I think I might know a way I can help you, but . . ."

My heart skipped in excitement. I felt like she was about to throw me a life raft, and I sat up straight.

"But what?"

"Well, the last thing you should probably do is get involved in more gambling," she said. "But . . ."

---

quandary: predicament   **propitious:** promising   **irony:** paradox
demeanor: outward manner

The muscles in my shoulders and neck coiled. More gambling? What was she talking about?

"Winter, what is it? I'm out of ideas here. If you can help . . ."

She sighed and shook her head. "I can't believe I'm going to do this, but here it is. My brother . . . you know my brother Gray."

I nodded. Gray had graduated a couple of years ago and went to our local community college.

"Well, he and his friends have a weekly game too," she said. "They play at my house, and they're not exactly the greatest players. Gray's friend Lenny is totally **obtuse**, and he has a **penchant** for going all in."

I knew the Lenny she was talking about. Lenny Racine. He had always been a total jerk to me when he went to Hillside, and I felt nothing but **antipathy** for the guy. Like Dominic, he would be someone I wouldn't mind winning money from.

"If you could get into their game . . . well, it might be a way out of **destitution**," she said

I don't think I had ever been more **enamored** of her than I was in that moment. Of course, there was one small flaw in the plan.

"Thanks, but I don't even have any money to bet with," I said.

"I could lend you some," Winter offered.

I snorted a laugh. "Thanks, but I don't want to be your **debtor**," I said. I was already in it up to my eyeballs with Ian. "What if I lost and couldn't **compensate** you? Somehow I don't think that would be good for our relationship."

It certainly hadn't been good for my relationship with Ian.

"Well, what else are you going to do?" Winter asked.

A very good question.

"I don't know," I replied.

"Well, what if you don't have to pay me back?" she asked.

"Yeah, right," I said.

"No! I'm serious!" Winter dropped down onto the bed, causing us both to bounce. "Look, it'll be my **philanthropic** act for the year,"

---

obtuse: dense
penchant: fondness
antipathy: dislike

destitution: poverty
enamored: fond
debtor: one who owes money

compensate: pay
philanthropic: charitable, generous

she said. "I'll lend you the money, and if you lose it, you won't have to pay it back, but that'll be it. It's going to be a one-time thing. That way we both know what the rules are going in. You won't ask me for more, and I won't be mad you lost my money because I know the risks."

I was tempted. Of course I was. But she was clearly nuts. "I can't do that," I said. "I can't just take your money."

"You're forgetting that if you win, you *will* be paying me back," she said. "It's only if you lose that I'm down. Have a little confidence, football star."

I looked at her in **awe**. How could I have possibly been so lucky to find someone this amazing?

"You're incredible, you know that?" I said.

She smiled. "Who's **espousing** my virtues now?" she joked. "But listen, you have to promise me something."

"Anything," I replied quickly.

"If you do lose the money, and I'm not saying you will, because, trust me, these guys are not the sharpest tools in the shed . . . But if you do, you have to tell your parents what's going on," she said. "You have to put an end to this."

Nothing filled me with more dread than the thought of confessing to my parents. I took a deep breath to try to **quell** the butterflies in my stomach and around my heart and finally nodded. If that was a condition she wanted to impose, then I would have to go with it. I had no other options.

"Fine," I said. "If I lose, I'll tell them. I promise."

She wrapped her arms around me and hugged me, and I stared past her at the football trophies over my bed. I knew that if I wanted Winter to trust me—if I had any chance of keeping her as my girlfriend—this promise was **irrevocable**. But it was also the last promise in the world I wanted to fulfill. I would just have to win. That was all there was to it. I *had* to win.

---

awe: amazement
espousing: supporting

quell: pacify

irrevocable: cannot be undone

"So, this is me," Winter said as I pulled my used car into her driveway on Saturday afternoon. "**Quaint**, isn't it?"

"It looks entirely different than the last time I was here," I said.

"I know. My mom completely **renovated** it," Winter replied. "And not for the better."

I stared out the window at the house, which was **commensurate** with my own. But that was where the similarities ended. Winter's place was a flower-laden cottage with a white picket fence and a lush green lawn. Yellow and orange flowers lined the walk to the house, and flower boxes hung from each and every window. A floral wreath hung on the door, and next to the door were two huge corn husks and a fake scarecrow, **undoubtedly** laid out to celebrate the fall season.

"My mom is kind of a flower freak," she explained. "Just . . . be prepared."

"All right then," I replied.

We got out of the car and she led me inside. I wiped the sweat from my brow with the back of my hand and told myself to chill. The fact that I was nervous wasn't a surprise. I was always nervous when walking into the house of a girl I liked. But today my **anxiety** wasn't over Winter's parents and winning their approval. It was over the three decks of cards I had hidden in various pockets of my jacket and jeans.

Yes, Mike Riley, one of the most **reputable** guys in Northern New York, was going to cheat. And Winter, although she didn't know it, was **abetting** my mission. That morning I had fed her a story about not wanting to be in my house—about how guilty I felt just being

---

quaint: charmingly old-fashioned
renovated: refurbished

commensurate: equal
undoubtedly: surely
anxiety: worry

reputable: esteemed
abetting: encouraging

around my parents. Which was totally true. But I had only complained about it in the hopes that she would ask me over. And she had. And now I could execute my plan.

I felt guilty about using her, of course. But at this point my guilt was so **compounded**, I couldn't even separate the causes anymore. And I had to do this. It was the only way to guarantee that I would win when I played her brother and his friends. It was the only way to guarantee that I could put an end to this nightmare and prevent my parents from losing all faith in me.

Winter opened the door to the house. "Okay, just don't judge," she said, her voice so low it was barely **audible**.

I stepped over the threshold and almost laughed. The floral theme outside was continued inside, but to a much greater extent. It looked like a flowerbed had thrown up inside her house. Pink-and-purple flowered wallpaper **adorned** the walls, and the living room was crowded with flowered rugs, flowered couches, and flowered pillows. The air was thick with some **saccharine** scent.

"Wow. It's . . . different," I said.

"Try not to heave," she told me. "It's a **quotidian** struggle for the rest of us."

I smirked and followed her into the kitchen. Here her mother was working a more **arboreal** theme. On one wall was painted a mural of a huge tree, its leaves hanging down around the windows by the table. The table and chairs themselves looked as if they were **fashioned** from branches and twigs. Collages of fall leaves were matted and framed over the cabinets.

"It's like *A Midsummer Night's Dream* in here. Is your mother a wood **sprite**?" I asked Winter, leaning back against the counter.

"That would explain *a lot*," Winter replied. "You want something to drink? A snack?"

"Sure," I replied.

---

compounded: combined into one	**adorned:** decorated	**arboreal:** treelike
audible: able to be heard	**saccharine:** overly sweet	**fashioned:** made
	quotidian: everyday	**sprite:** elf

"Okay, why don't you go downstairs? It's much more normal down there," she said, opening the fridge. "I'll be down in a sec."

Downstairs. The basement. Most likely where Gray and his friends played their games. Normally I would have stayed and helped Winter bring down the food, but this was the perfect opportunity to carry out my plan.

"Where do I go?" I asked.

"Door's right there," she replied, gesturing over her shoulder. "Light switch is at the top of the stairs."

I took a deep breath and headed down to the basement. The stairs creaked under my weight, and my heart pounded as I reached the cool cement floor. Old leather couches were set up around a trodden shag rug, facing a big-screen television. The walls were lined with built-in bookcases that were packed to the gills with old volumes, board games, and knickknacks. I scanned the room quickly and, much to my relief, found exactly what I was hoping for. Leaning against the wall was a folding table—strictly **utilitarian**, unlike Ian's state-of-the-art poker table—and next to it was a sideboard that held all the poker **paraphernalia**. The chip box was right there, and next to it, right in plain sight, a deck of cards.

Hands quaking, I grabbed the deck and checked it over. Thank God Gray wasn't using unique cards. They were a standard deck with blue checks on the back. I pulled out a royal and checked it against a royal card from the blue deck I had brought. A perfect match.

The door at the top of the stairs opened, and I quickly dropped Gray's cards, tucking my own back into my pocket. Then I grabbed the remote and flicked on the television. Winter appeared with a tray full of chips, salsa, and melted cheese and a big bottle of Coke, plus a brand new bag of Oreos.

I sat down on the couch, hoping she wouldn't notice I was all flushed. "Wow. You guys really have all the **amenities** around here, huh?" I said as she placed the food on the coffee table.

---

utilitarian: simple and useful

paraphernalia: equipment

amenities: conveniences

"Mom may have been in charge of the décor, but Dad is the one who buys the snacks," she said. "And when it comes to snacks, he does not mess around."

I glanced around as if for the first time. Getting myself into this ridiculous **morass** had really helped me improve my **subterfuge** abilities. Not sure if that was a good thing or a bad thing.

"Is there a bathroom where I can wash up?" I asked.

"Yeah. Right back there," Winter replied, stuffing a chip in her mouth.

Perfect. A bathroom **accessible** from the poker room. This was working out even better than I'd hoped. I walked into the small, **antiseptic** room and closed the door behind me. I just wanted to get this over with so I could stop feeling so tense and jittery. I needed a hiding space—someplace I could stash the cards until tomorrow night's game. Someplace no one would disturb before then.

I thought about placing the deck at the bottom of the garbage pail, but it was half full and someone might empty it. I checked the tissue box, but it wouldn't fit. I was just about to start panicking when I noticed a long, skinny door behind me. I yanked it open. Inside were stacks of towels and washcloths. This was clearly a guest bathroom. So unless they were going to have guests tonight, this was the perfect hiding place. I slipped the deck out of my pocket and tucked it back behind a set of lime-green towels—flowered, of course. Then I folded a washcloth over it, just to be safe.

I closed the closet up and was just relaxing when there was a loud knock on the bathroom door.

"Dude! What're you doing in there?!"

It was Gray. This was not a good **portent**.

"I'll . . . I'll be right out," I replied.

I ran the water quickly, dried my shaking hands, and stared at myself in the mirror. The light **refracted** off a flaw in the glass,

---

morass: difficult situation   **antiseptic:** extremely clean   **refracted:** reflected
subterfuge: trickery   **portent:** omen   distortedly
accessible: within reach

making my face seem as if it were split down the middle—disturbing. Taking a deep breath, I opened the door.

Gray was bigger than I remembered. And he did not look happy. His blue eyes were narrowed in suspicion under his red baseball cap, and he looked down his nose at me, his hands tucked under his biceps. I'm a tall guy—there aren't many people who could look *down* at me—and I found it more than a little disconcerting. Had he somehow seen me come in here? Was I so **negligent** that I didn't notice someone else in the room? Could he have possibly known what I had done?

"'Sup?" Gray said.

"Hey, man," I said.

"I hear you think you can get into my Sunday night game," he said. "Little **presumptuous** of you, don't you think?"

Practically shaking in my sneakers, I shot Winter a panicked look over his huge shoulder. She just rolled her eyes. Was this really a time for rolling the eyes?

"I . . . uh . . . didn't. Winter said—"

Apparently Gray's intimidating **veneer**, coupled with my recent crime, had **obfuscated** my ability to speak.

"I—"

Suddenly Gray broke out into a huge smile. "I'm just messing with you man," he said, bringing a beefy hand down on my shoulder. "Of course you can get into my game. The guys'll be psyched to have you."

I was so relieved I could have collapsed. Gray jostled me out of the bathroom and into the common area.

"Now, let's talk about that kickass performance of yours last night," he said amiably. "You had Tony Odewale eating your dust. How the hell did that *feel*?"

I laughed as we all sat down on the couch together. Nothing like a narrow escape to make a guy feel very, very good.

---

negligent: neglectful   **veneer:** façade   **obfuscated:** confused
presumptuous: assuming

*   *   *   *   *

"Hey! Look who it is! The man of the hour!"

Gray stood up from the couch where he and his friends were playing on his Xbox 360. Unlike the day before, the basement was **noisome** and thick with cigar smoke. I tried not to cough as Gray stuffed his cigar in his mouth and greeted me with a one-armed hug. If I was going to have to be inhaling this crap, this night was going to be even longer than I anticipated.

"Hey, man," I said, breathing through my mouth.

"You know the guys, right?" he said, keeping his arm around me. "Lenny Racine."

"What's up?" Lenny **muttered**, lifting his chin, but keeping his eyes trained on the TV. His black hair was slicked back from his face, as **unctuous** as I remembered it. Lenny was one of those guys who was always rocking the *Sopranos* style. As I recalled, he enjoyed constantly pointing out other people's shortcomings and picking on anyone smaller and less tough than himself. I never understood why Gray was friends with him.

"Rick Boscow."

Rick, a scrawny guy with red hair and freckles who had played fourth-string receiver a couple of years ago, got up from the couch and shook my hand.

"Hey, Mike. Nice game the other night. You were like some **maverick** out there. What did you do, make up half those plays yourself?" he asked.

"No. They were in the playbook," I replied. "Most of them, anyway."

Rick laughed. "Wish we'd had you playing quarterback when I was on the team," he said **obsequiously**. "You think you guys are going all the way this year?"

"Maybe," I replied. "We'll see."

---

noisome: noxious	**unctuous:** oily	**obsequiously:** obediently
muttered: murmured	**maverick:** rebel	

Rick was an **affable** guy, but he had always been kind of **malleable**, which wasn't my favorite characteristic in a person. Whatever Gray said, went. He was a total follower. His cigar sat in an ashtray in front of him and looked as if it hadn't been touched. He had probably only taken one because all the other guys had.

"And, of course, Ogre," Gray said.

Ogre—whose real name was Todd Ogretski—lifted his large hand for a punch. I touched my fist to his. Neither of us said anything. Ogre was **renowned** for his silence. He barely ever spoke, and when he did, it was almost always in **platitudes**. Back when he was the leading linebacker on our team, the only things I had ever heard him say were "We play to win" and "The glory is not in never falling, but in rising every time we fall." Stuff like that.

"So, what have you guys been up to since graduation?" I asked.

"I've been working at my dad's shop, taking some classes at the community college on the side," Lenny answered. His father owned one of the bigger auto body shops in the area. "Ogre mainly sits around and sucks his parents dry."

Ogre picked up a plastic cup and chucked it at Lenny. It bounced off Lenny's head and hit the floor.

"Hey! Watch the hair!" Lenny said.

"Lenny's hair is **sacrosanct**," Gray said.

I laughed. "What about you, Rick?" I asked.

"I'm going to SUNY Binghamton," he said proudly. "Just home for the weekend."

"*And* he's a total **partisan** of Hillside football," Gray said, puffing on his cigar. "Guy still cuts out every article written about you guys. He's totally **mawkish** for the old days."

"I am not," Rick protested, turning beet red under his freckles. "I just like to follow the team. I think it's cool to be into your alma mater."

"Yeah. I love it when alumni come to games," I said.

---

affable: gracious   **platitudes:** dull remarks   **partisan:** follower
malleable: easily influenced   **sacrosanct:** sacred   **mawkish:** overly sentimental
renowned: widely known

"Please. Don't encourage him," Lenny said, his thumbs pounding away at his controller. "The guy lives **vicariously** through you."

Rick ignored him. "Have you seen some of the stuff they write about you, Mike? You're totally **revered** around here."

"I don't know about that," I said, growing embarrassed.

"How's the new coach? I hear he's **punctilious**, but it seems to be working," Rick said. "Do you think you guys'll beat Dorchester next weekend?"

"I—"

"I think Gary Robinson is the best running back in the division. How're you guys gonna shut him down?"

"Aw, man! Leave the kid alone!" Lenny said, standing. He paused his game and threw the controller down. "See? You were too **accommodating**, and now this little idiot's never gonna shut up," he said to me, whacking Rick on the back of the head so that his hair stood up.

"Ow!" Rick protested. "I was just asking a couple of questions."

"Maybe you should give him something," Gray said with a smile. "Throw him an **anecdote** from Friday night's game, and then we can get on with things."

I noticed that everyone was looking at me with interest—even Ogre and Lenny. These guys played on the mediocre teams that were an **antecedent** to our current success. Now I had everything they had wanted back in their glory days. So I obliged. I sat down and told them all about the game on Friday—what it was like to be on the field and face down Westmont. It was the least I could do, considering I was planning on cheating them out of their hard earned cash—if I *had* to—as soon as humanly possible.

*   *   *   *   *

---

vicariously: by proxy
revered: honored
punctilious: strict

accommodating: considerate

anecdote: brief story
antecedent: predecessor

An hour later, we had played three hands, and almost all the money Winter had lent me was gone. I would love to say that, once again, the cards were not in my favor, but this time I had to take some of the blame. I had underestimated my opponents. Winter's **pejorative** comments about Lenny's game had turned out to be dead on. I could practically **catalog** every **nuance** of his many tells and each of his betting tendencies already—but the other guys weren't all that bad. And they had taken all the pots.

I glanced at my dwindling chips and at my cards, trying to maintain a **staid** appearance. If I didn't win this hand, it would be my **penultimate** one. I had just enough money to play one more and then I would be broke and have to tell my parents what I'd been up to. That was not an option. Aside from cheating, all I could do was pray, and I'd already done a lot of that. I'd prayed for a queen on the first hand, a two on the second, and a jack on the third. Not a single one had been answered. Honestly, I was starting to think I should become an atheist. Or at the very least, an **agnostic**.

I took a deep breath and scanned the cards as Ogre laid out his bet. All I needed for a straight was a three, but I didn't have it. The river was about to be dealt, and I wouldn't be able to leave the room after that. It would be too obvious. If I was going to act, it would have to be now.

"Dealing the river," Gray said.

"You guys, I'm sorry, but I gotta go to the bathroom," I said.

"No one leaves the table in the middle of a game," Lenny replied automatically, shifting in his seat.

"What? Like Mike Riley is going to cheat," Rick said with a guffaw. His trust in me made me feel totally **reprobate**. What kind of disgusting jerk was I, crashing this game and then cheating these guys? But one more look at my pitiful chips **assuaged** my self-loathing. This was about survival. A guy had to do what a guy had to do.

---

pejorative: negative
catalog: list
nuance: variation

staid: serious
penultimate: second-to-last
agnostic: unsure of the existence of God

reprobate: morally corrupt
assuaged: eased

"No one leaves the table in the middle of a game," Lenny repeated through his teeth.

Damn, he was scary when that vein in his forehead started to throb. And now he was totally suspicious of me. If I ever did get up from this table, which wasn't looking good, and I did get the card I needed, I would have to make absolutely sure I wasn't caught. Otherwise I'd be on the lam by the end of the night, trying to come up with a good **alias**.

"Dude, let the kid take a piss," Gray said. "Look at him. He's gonna make on the floor."

I guess my extreme tension was written all over my face.

Lenny blew out a sigh. "Fine. But he leaves his hole cards here."

My throat went dry. "Fine," I said, standing.

I walked on shaky legs over to the bathroom. Behind me, I could hear them whispering and wondered if they were scolding Lenny or speculating about me—trying to **ascertain** whether I was capable of messing with them. Probably a little bit of both.

Inside the bathroom I leaned against the sink and tried to breathe. I stared at myself in the mirror and realized I did look pained and rather pale. What was I thinking? I couldn't go through with this. Especially not now. Now that Lenny had called me out, those guys were going to be keeping their hawk eyes on me every second. I would never get away with it.

But you have to, a little voice in my head warned me. *You have to do this or you're done. Your life is over.*

I felt hot and sick to my stomach. All the cigar smoke and junk food was not helping. I stood there for another long moment, **vacillating** between one option and the other. Cheat now and risk getting the crap kicked out of me, or don't cheat and risk putting my parents through some serious pain. It was thinking about my mother that made up my mind. I thought about her and everything she had done for me. I thought about the way she would react when she found

---

alias: fake name   **ascertain:** figure out   **vacillating:** wavering

out what I had done. And as soon as I conjured up an image of her face, I knew I had to **adhere** to the plan.

Before I could rethink it, I flushed the toilet, opened the closet, and fumbled for the cards. I flipped through them, pulled out the one I needed, and shoved it up my sleeve. Then I tucked the **superfluous** cards back in their hiding spot. I would come back for them later—after the night was over.

If I lived that long.

*　*　*　*　*

I gotta say, winning is my personal **panacea**. As I approached Ian's **behemoth** of a house later that night, I had gone through an extreme **metamorphosis**. I no longer felt like a **pariah**. I no longer felt like some loser with no control and no skills. I was back, baby. On the road to redemption. And it felt good.

I took a deep breath of the cold night air and watched as the steam exhaled from my mouth. Everything felt better. Even *breathing* felt good. I rang the doorbell and waited while its **melodious** tune echoed through the lofty halls of Ian's house. As expected, it was Ian who answered the door. In my entire life, neither of his parents had ever been the ones to answer the door. My own parents sometimes doubted that the O'Connors even existed.

Ian looked confused when he saw me standing on his front step. Not that I'm surprised. It was rather late on a Sunday, and we hadn't spoken in days. He shivered against the cold and stepped back so that I could come in. It wasn't much warmer in the marble hall behind the front door.

"Hey, man," Ian said a little coolly. "What's up?"

"I am here to make **restitution**," I said grandly.

From my back pocket I pulled out a wad of cash. Ian's reaction did not disappoint. He was absolutely **stupefied**. I wasn't sure

---

adhere: stick
superfluous: extra
panacea: cure-all
behemoth: something huge

metamorphosis:
transformation
pariah: outcast

melodious: musical
restitution: payback
stupefied: astonished

whether to feel **aggrieved** by this fact. Did he really think that I was never going to pay him back?

But I decided to ignore it. I was not here for an **altercation**. I was here to make amends.

"Where the hell did you get all that?" Ian asked.

"**Abridged** version? I was hot tonight, man," I said, quickly counting through the bills.

"Hot tonight? Hot tonight where? Did you play poker?" Ian asked. He almost sounded **petulant**—upset that I had played without him. When *he* was the one who had barred me from his game. *Sheesh*.

"Yeah, I did," I said. "And I won. Here. This is the money I've **allocated** for you. I think you'll find it's all there."

He took the bills from my hand in wonder. "Damn, man."

"I know. Cool, huh?" I said, grinning. "I know it's **belated**, but—"

"No. I'm not psyched about the money," he said. Then, when my face fell, he added, "I mean, thanks for paying me back, but . . . I just can't believe you're still playing."

I felt a lump form in my chest. Usually I'm pretty **resilient**, but I'd had enough of his negative attitude. I couldn't believe he was attacking me just then. When I had come over there to make up. Our relationship was **contentious** enough as it was. Couldn't he recognize an olive branch when he saw it?

"Dude, I cleaned up tonight. I played with Gray Dumas and his friends—all those guys we used to look up to—and I won," I told him. "I came over her to tell you what happened and maybe celebrate with you, and instead you're acting like I did something wrong."

Of course, I *had* done something wrong. I had done something *very* wrong. I had managed to slip that three into my hand and had won the pot. And after that I was unstoppable. I had won another, and another, until finally the other guys had to bow out. I had been

aggrieved: wronged	**petulant:** peeved	**resilient:** able to adapt
altercation: quarrel	**allocated:** set aside	**contentious:** argumentative
abridged: shortened	**belated:** late	

at the **pinnacle** of my game. And that little sleight of hand was what had turned it all around.

Which was not the point, of course. The point was I *had* turned it around. I had won every other hand fair and square. And I was proud of myself.

Ian looked down at the money and sighed again. "You're right, Mike. I'm sorry," he said finally. "It's just, I was—"

"Worried about me. I know," I said. I took a deep breath and looked at him. "Would it help if I swore I was never going to play another game?"

Ian's eyes lit up. "Seriously?"

"Yeah, seriously," I said with a shrug. "It's no big deal. It's not like I was addicted to it or something. I just needed to get my money back. Which I did."

"You won *all* of it back?" Ian asked.

I swallowed hard. "Well . . . yeah," I lied. In actuality, after paying Winter and Ian back I only had a couple hundred—not nearly enough to restore my balance. But Ian didn't need to know that. I fully intended to play with Gray and the guys again—I'd play until I got it all back—but he didn't need to know that either. A couple white lies were nothing between friends. This way he wouldn't have to keep "worrying" about me, and I wouldn't have to keep feeling him looking over my shoulder.

"So, we cool?" I asked.

Ian smiled. "Yeah. We're cool," he replied.

"Good."

I was just going to have to be **vigilant** around him. Keep my money and my thoughts to myself until I got it all back. Then things would finally be able to go back to normal.

---

pinnacle: peak   **vigilant:** cautious

Chapter Ten

As I walked home after football practice later that week, I was feeling better than I had in a long time. I had deposited some money back into my savings account, and my parents had yet to notice the late statement, so I still had time to rebuild my balance. If I could just make it through the weekend and the next game with Gray and his friends, I would be golden. I ducked through the fence that ran around the playing fields and hit the path that led through the **grove** and straight to the street where I lived. As I walked, I whipped out my cell to call Winter, hoping that we could have another movie night. I was so **distracted** with dialing that I didn't notice anyone else on the path until I was practically on top of them.

"Hey."

My heart seized at the sound of the **gruff** voice, and I stopped **abruptly**. Standing right in my path were Gray, Lenny, and Ogre, who looked **gargantuan** standing next to his friends. Instantly, all the hairs on the back of my neck stood on end. They formed a **daunting** trio, and they did not look happy.

They know, I realized. And suddenly I wished I had taken up my friends from the offensive line when they had asked if I wanted to join them for pizza. Or that, at the very least, a couple of those guys were here **flanking** me right now. They acted as great **buttresses** during games, and at the moment, I knew I could use a couple of bodyguards.

"What's up, guys?" I asked casually, playing it off as if we met this way every day.

"You tell us," Ogre said, stepping forward. "You tell us how the great Mike Riley could turn out to be such a rat."

---

grove: area of trees
distracted: diverted
gruff: husky

abruptly: suddenly
gargantuan: huge
daunting: intimidating

flanking: bordering
buttresses: supports

Apparently his usual quiet was just an **affectation**. **Embezzle** some money from the guy and he finds all kinds of words.

"What do you mean?" I asked, starting to sweat.

"Don't try to play innocent, Riley," Gray said. "We know you cheated."

Oh God. I was dead. My life was actually flashing before my eyes, and it wasn't pretty. I glanced around, wondering if there was any way I could **flee**, but it was no use. There was no way I could navigate all the rocks and trees and fallen branches and get away. One of these guys would surely catch up with me.

"That's a serious **allegation**," I said, grasping at straws—stalling for time. How had they found out? *How?*

Gray pulled something out of his back pocket and everything inside of me sunk. He had two blue playing cards in his hand. Where had they come from? How could I have been so careless?

"You're pretty good. They're exact **duplicates**," Gray said. "Just like the deck we always use."

"Here's a tip," Lenny said, stepping up next to me. He was so close I could smell onions on his breath. "If you're going to try to cheat someone out of their money, don't leave such **incriminating** evidence behind."

He grabbed the cards out of Gray's hand and flung them at my feet. My heart pounded in every inch of my body. Trying to explain anything to them was **futile**, I knew. With evidence like that, there was no way I could **exculpate** myself. All I could do was throw myself at their mercy and hope they would be **benevolent**.

"Listen, guys. I'm really sorry—"

My sentence was cut short as I was suddenly, violently, shoved back against a thick oak tree. My head slammed into the rough bark, and I saw stars. For a good few seconds, I couldn't breathe. They were going to kill me. They had come here to kill me.

---

affectation: pose	**allegation**: accusation	**futile**: useless
embezzle: swindle	**duplicates**: copies	**exculpate**: clear from guilt
flee: escape	**incriminating**: proving guilt	**benevolent**: kind

"I knew we shouldn't've let this asswipe get up from the table," Lenny said as he held my shoulder back so far I screamed out in pain. "Why do you guys always gotta **challenge** me?"

"I don't know what pisses me off more. The fact that you cheated, or the fact that you used my little sister to do it," Gray said, squaring off in front of me.

"It's . . . it's not like that," I said quickly.

"Oh, no? Then what's it like?" Ogre demanded, twisting my arm back. I cried out in pain and bit my lip. So much for an **amicable** solution to this mess.

"Here's the deal, superstar," Gray said. He picked up a thick branch from the ground and **brandished** it. "You pay us back every dime, and we won't kill you."

I choked, finally sucking in wind, and tried to double over, but Ogre and Lenny held me fast. For all the strength in my well-conditioned body, I couldn't move a muscle.

"I . . . I can't," I said, barely **coherent**. "I don't . . . have . . . the money."

Lenny pulled back one hand and slammed his fist right into my gut. I wheezed for air and clouds formed over my eyes. This was worse than any hit I had ever taken in a game. I thought I was going to pass out, but finally the pain **ebbed**, and I was able to breathe again. Even as I fought for air, my brain tried to figure some way— any way—out of this mess. Could I **divert** their attention somehow and make a run for it? Hardly seemed likely, considering I could barely breathe. What could I say that would be in any way **conciliatory**? How could I get them to back off?

"How could you not have it?" Gray asked, stepping forward.

"I . . . I paid some people back," I told him, my eyes pleading for mercy. "I wouldn't have even cheated except that I was already in debt," I added, hoping to **convey** my desperation, hoping they would take pity on me. "I just don't have it, Gray. I'm sorry."

---

challenge: disagree with
amicable: friendly
brandished: held as a weapon

coherent: sensible
ebbed: eased
divert: redirect

conciliatory: appeasing
convey: pass on

I felt like I was about to cry, but I knew that was the last thing I could do in front of these guys. That kind of **degradation** would only make them want to hurt me more.

Gray looked at his friends as if for guidance, and I felt a surge of hope. Maybe he believed me. Maybe he was backing down!

"Well, then you'd better figure out a way to get it back," he said finally, **embittered**. "We're not just gonna let this slide, Riley. And I'm assuming that you're gonna want to keep your all-star legs intact. A shattered shin, for example, wouldn't do much for your prospects."

He pulled back as if to slam me with the branch, and I screamed. "No! No! No! Wait! I have an idea!"

Gray stopped, and a couple of tears squeezed out. Lenny clucked his tongue in clear disgust.

"I have an idea," I repeated. And, in fact, I did. It was amazing how intense fear inspired creativity.

"I'm listening," Gray said, leaning on the branch now as if it were just a benign walking stick.

"What if I . . . what if I throw the game this weekend?" I asked.

That got their attention. "The big rivalry game?" Ogre asked.

"Yeah," I replied, desperate. "You guys bet on the game, and I'll take a dive. Then you can win back your money and then some. It'll be a sure thing."

"You'd do that?" Lenny asked, amazed. "You'd lay down to Dorchester?"

I swallowed hard. This was the biggest game of my life. A source of major pride for me, the team, and the school. Throwing the game would mean letting all those people down. Plus, Coach had told me that scouts from a few major football powerhouses were coming that weekend to check me out. Including, quite possibly, Penn State—although it hadn't been confirmed. Taking a dive could keep me from **attaining** all the things I had worked so hard for my entire

---

degradation: humiliation   **embittered:** bitter   **attaining:** achieving

life, but then, what would any of that matter if I were paralyzed, maimed, or dead?

"To keep you guys from killing me, yeah," I said.

Gray took a deep breath. "Seems like an **equitable** solution to me," he said with a shrug. His **flippancy** made me crazy, but it wasn't as if I could say anything. "Let him go."

Ogre and Lenny released me, and my quaking knees somehow supported me. I was still scared out of my mind. There was a good chance I wasn't going to feel safe again until I got home and locked the door behind me. Maybe not even then.

"We're in," Gray said, looking down his nose at me. Ogre and Lenny gathered in close, breathing down my neck. "Now don't let us down."

Seemingly **innocuous** words, but they may as well have been a death threat.

"I won't," I promised them, my voice trembling. "I swear to you, I won't."

*   *   *   *   *

"I don't believe this. Tell me you're kidding. Please just tell me you're messing with me."

I sat there on the end of my bed and watched as Winter stood up and started to pace. After much **circumlocution**, I had finally managed to tell her what I had done and how her brother had reacted. I had wanted to confess before Gray had a chance to tell her and **exaggerate** the seriousness of my crime. But seeing Winter's reaction, I knew that what I had done needed no exaggeration to be deemed utterly **reprehensible** and that it could possibly even be the final blow to our already delicate relationship.

"You used me," she said, turning an **accusatory** glare on me.

"I didn't," I replied automatically. "I just—"

---

equitable: fair
flippancy: cheek, frivolity

innocuous: harmless, trivial
circumlocution: talking in circles

exaggerate: overstate
reprehensible: disgraceful
accusatory: blaming

"Came with me into my house and planted a deck of cards in my bathroom so that you could cheat my brother and his friends," Winter pointed out, summing things up **concisely**. "What would you call that?"

Okay. So I was every bit as **devious** as she said. "I'm . . . I'm sorry," I said. "There were **extenuating** circumstances, okay? I didn't *want* to cheat. I just—"

"Oh my God! Do you even hear yourself?" Winter cried, pushing her hands through her hair. "What do you expect? Do you expect me to tell you that I **endorse** this kind of thing? That I wanted you to win by whatever means necessary?"

"No! But you *did* give me certain **assurances** about how bad they were at poker," I said. "I mean, you did want me to win—"

"But not this way!" Winter replied, **impassioned**. "Do you even know who you're messing with here? Screwing over my brother and his friends is sheer **lunacy**. They're not patient people, Mike. They'll kick your ass and ask questions later. If they even *bother* to ask questions. My brother lives for his reputation as a **firebrand**."

Yeah. No duh. I had found that out the hard way. "I get that now. Trust me."

Suddenly, her entire face changed. She sat down next to me as if the wind were knocked out of her. "Oh, God. They don't think I was in **collusion** with you, do they?" she asked, her eyes wide.

"No. They don't," I replied. "Why? It's not like your brother would hurt you," I said, then gulped. "Is it?"

"No," she said with a sigh, looking relieved. "But if he thought I helped you it certainly wouldn't **enhance** my quality of living."

"I'm really sorry, Winter," I told her, **contrite**.

She looked down at her hands, folded in her lap, and I knew she was wondering what to do—wondering if I were worth all this trouble. Suddenly I felt a wave of panic pass through me. I had already lost everything. If Winter left me, I didn't know what I would do.

concisely: sharply	**assurances:** promises	**collusion:** secret agreement
devious: cunning	**impassioned:** excited	**enhance:** increase
extenuating: mitigating	**lunacy:** madness	**contrite:** sorry
endorse: support	**firebrand:** troublemaker	

But I did know that I wouldn't blame her for going. What reason had I given her to stick it out?

"Do you see it now?" Winter asked. "Do you see how **corrosive** gambling is?"

I blinked. Winter had never said anything like this to me before. She sounded like Ian. For a split second I felt my ire flare up. She was **censuring** me too? But then I realized that after everything that happened, she had every right to accuse me. The **banality** of my situation was abundantly clear. I was a cliché. One of those kids you hear about on the news—a "victim of the poker trend." One of those losers who get **entangled** in a web of debt and can't pull himself out. One of those kids I always pitied.

"I know," I said finally. "I'm an idiot."

She didn't disagree with me. "What're you going to do? I mean, I know Gray's gonna make you pay him back, but did you at least ask him for a **deferment**? Maybe he can wait until you get your part-time job in the winter. Maybe you guys can do some kind of payment plan or something."

I almost laughed. As well as she seemed to know her brother, she apparently thought he was a little more **compassionate** and reasonable than he was.

"He made it fairly clear that immediate repayment was **essential**," I replied. *Essential if I wanted to continue to breathe,* I thought with a shudder. "So I came up with a plan . . ."

Winter regarded me with concern. "What kind of plan?"

"You're not gonna like it," I told her.

She cleared her throat and squared her shoulders, pulling her leg up on the bed so she could face me. "Hit me."

So I told her. I told her all about the plan to throw the Dorchester game, and although Winter had always been rather **ambivalent** when it came to both football and school spirit, she flinched when I **divulged** the details. By the time I was done, she was staring at me

---

corrosive: damaging
censuring: scolding
banality: ordinary nature
entangled: trapped
deferment: temporary delay
compassionate: sympathetic
essential: necessary
ambivalent: undecided, conflicted
divulged: revealed

as if she were ready to make the call to the nearest **asylum**. At that point, I would have gone willingly. A few days of peace and quiet and four **drab** walls was probably exactly what I needed. Plus, I'd be safe from Gray and his **cantankerous** goons.

"Mike, you can't," she said slowly. "What about your future? What about the other guys on the team?"

"I know. It's not as if I didn't think about that," I told her. "Believe me. It's *all* I think about. But I have no choice. It's either this or your brother kicks the crap out of me."

She knew him well enough that she kept her mouth shut at that, which did not make me feel better. But at that point I think I was beyond feeling better. I had gotten myself into this horrible situation, and there was only one way to get myself out.

* * * * *

It wasn't until the day of the rivalry game that I understood with complete **clarity** the depth of the crime I was about to commit. As my friends and teammates readied for the game around me, all I could think about was how I was about to **betray** them. I loathed myself. But I couldn't even show it. My behavior had to be **concordant** with that of my friends. I had to act all psyched like we were about to put a beat-down on our number-one nemesis, while all the time I was plotting *against* my team.

"These losers are going down!" Curtis Springer cheered.

"Yeah!" I shouted **emphatically**, my voice blending with those of my teammates. A bunch of guys laughed and smiled confidently at me, the guy who was supposed to take them to the promised land. I felt like the biggest heel in the world.

"Hey, man. Coach wants to see you," Daryl said, slapping my arm as he sat down next to me to tie his cleats. "He probably wants to make sure his golden boy hasn't started to believe his own hype," he joked.

---

asylum: mental institution
drab: colorless
cantankerous: cranky

clarity: clearness
betray: prove unfaithful to

concordant: agreeing
emphatically: with emphasis

I smiled, but I felt nauseated as I stood up. I could see the head-lines now. "Star Quarterback Chokes!" " **Incompetent** Riley Leads Cardinals to Defeat!" "Scouts Tell Riley 'No Thanks!'" My future, which had seemed so bright a few days ago, was now **ambiguous**. All thanks to one stupid game of poker. Well, a few stupid games. I couldn't remotely **comprehend** how I had ended up here.

I knocked quickly on the coach's door, and he waved me in. I so wanted to **expedite** this whole day—to flash forward to the end of the game so I could just go home and crawl under the covers.

"Hey, Coach. Daryl said you wanted to see me," I said.

He was practically glowing with pride and anticipation. "This is it, Mike. All your **assiduousness** is about to pay off."

My throat was dry. I felt heavy with guilt and dread.

"Coach?" I said. I couldn't trust myself to utter more than one word.

"Guess which schools sent scouts out to **evaluate** you today. Just guess," he told me.

I didn't want to guess. But I would have done anything to **curtail** this meeting and the misery it was bringing on.

"Uh . . . I don't know," I said.

"Everyone who's anyone," he said, clearly beside himself with glee. "Those bleachers are going to be hosting a **convergence** of some of the biggest reps in the country. USC. Michigan. Texas."

With each school named, I grew more and more depressed.

"And, of course, Penn State," he said finally.

Now I was definitely going to throw up.

"Did you hear me, Mike?" Coach asked.

I cleared my throat. "Yeah, Coach," I said. "That's great."

"When you look back on this day, you are going to realize that it was **decisive** in determining the course of your life," Coach said, laying it on so thick I felt like I was suffocating. "I don't think it would be presumptuous of me to say that if you go out there today

---

incompetent: without skill   expedite: speed up   curtail: shorten
ambiguous: vague   assiduousness: diligence   convergence: gathering
comprehend: understand   evaluate: assess   decisive: conclusive

and play the way I know you can play, you are going to be entertaining some **immoderate** offers tonight."

I couldn't believe he was saying these things to me. Even if I wasn't planning on throwing the game, putting this much pressure on me would surely be **debilitating**. Who could hold up under such high expectations? Who could live up to such ideals?

You could have, a little voice in my mind chided me. *You could have had it all.*

I **disregarded** the voice. I couldn't focus on some **indeterminate** moment in my potential future—some moment at which I would look back on today and realize how much it had meant. Right now all I could think about was living long enough to see tomorrow. And unfortunately that meant risking my entire future.

"Are you ready for this, Mike?" Coach asked. He had so many stars in his eyes that apparently he couldn't see that his quarterback was turning green right in front of him.

"Yes, Coach," I said.

There was a knock on the door, and his assistant, Coach Nimenen, stuck his head in. "Sorry to **encroach**, Coach, but it's time."

I stood up slowly, shakily. It was time, all right. Time to finish this once and for all.

---

immoderate: excessive	**disregarded:** ignored	**encroach:** trespass
debilitating: weakening	**indeterminate:** unknown	

"Come on, Riley! You're killing me!" Coach shouted from the sidelines. "Watch the damn blitz!"

Joe Trung, Dorchester's lead linebacker, shoved me a little farther into the ground as he pushed himself up. This guy, who would have been totally **nondescript** if you saw him on the street, was a menace on the football field, and all I had done all day was hover in his path and let him take me down.

It was getting kind of **strenuous**, to say the least. But that's what I got for abandoning all **rectitude** and turning to the dark side.

Curtis came over and offered me his hand, but I shook my head. The offer was nothing if not kind and only augmented my guilt. The last thing I wanted right now was to let my teammates help me out. Not when I was, unbeknownst to them, stabbing them in the back.

I pulled myself up out of the mud and muck and shook my hands, flinging grime everywhere. It was the second quarter and the crowd had grown **vociferous**, but not in a good way. I had a feeling that as soon as the ref blew the whistle to signal halftime, the stands were going to empty out and the fans were going to bring their **wrath** down on me. And why not? Anyone who was keeping a **vigilant** eye on my game could **impute** the blame to no one other than the quarterback. We were losing 17 to 3 and were now moving backward, thanks to penalties and sacks. I was engineering the perfect loss, and with each passing moment, more and more **maledictions** rained down on me from our diehard fans.

I groaned as I joined the guys in the huddle. Trung had slammed me pretty hard on that last play. There was a **laceration** on my arm that was throbbing with pain and bleeding pretty profusely, even

nondescript: indistinct	**vociferous:** vocal	**impute:** attribute
strenuous: exhausting	**wrath:** anger	**maledictions:** curses
rectitude: righteousness	**vigilant:** alert	**laceration:** cut

though it was matted with mud and grass. Daryl checked it out as he stepped next to me.

"Maybe you should have Dick clean that up," he said. "Looks pretty bad."

Dick Carerri, our trainer, was watching me with concern from the sideline.

"I'm fine," I said. In fact, the injury sort of felt like penance for how I was **desecrating** this team, our stadium, our entire season. Let it bleed until I dropped. I deserved it.

"All right, guys. We're gonna go to the sidelines on this one. Twenty-two sweep," I said, feeling like evil **incarnate**. I knew there was no way running wide would be **efficacious** in this game. These guys had studied our tape and were expecting us to run this play, which was clear considering they had moved their most **lithe** tackle to the strong side. All the better to stop our running back, Tommy Jasper, if he decided to go wide.

I saw a couple of guys in the huddle exchange a look. They knew the play had no chance as well, but they were too **deferential** to me to say anything. I didn't know how they could **abide** my total **ineptness** today. I almost wished someone *would* call me out. I would have thought more of them if they did. On top of which, the guilt was becoming overwhelming.

"Okay. Ready? Break!"

We moved out of the huddle to the line. As I dropped down behind my center, I wondered if anyone had figured out that I was **deliberately** driving us into the ground—if they knew that their star quarterback was just allowing Dorchester to **usurp** our position at the top of the league. I felt like it was so obvious it may as well have been written across the back of my jersey: "Traitor, #3." The quality of my play was that much of an **anomaly**. But no one seemed suspicious. They just seemed confused. Apparently, they all trusted me. Which only made me feel worse.

---

desecrating: profaning
incarnate: in the flesh
efficacious: effective
lithe: gracefully athletic

deferential: respectful
abide: tolerate
ineptness: incompetence

deliberately: purposefully
usurp: take over
anomaly: irregularity

"Blue eighty! Blue eighty!" I shouted.

Dorchester's **dynamic** defense shifted, picking up on our formation. A **cursory** look at their new line would have told any competent quarterback to change the play with an audible—to call a pass. But I didn't.

"Hike!"

The ball hit my hands, and I handed it off to Tommy Jasper. About two seconds later he was crushed by the tremendous defensive tackle. The helmet-against-helmet crack was loud enough to draw a groan from both crowds.

As Dorchester's lineman stood up with his fists raised to the air, Curtis ran over and shoved him, slamming him back into the ground. Suddenly both teams were on top of each other in a brawl, going at each other **insatiably**. For a split second I just stood there, stunned. I guess my team got a little **bellicose** when they were being thrashed by our archrivals.

I saw Daryl get smashed across the facemask, and I snapped into action, running for the **melee**. But one of the refs jumped in and held me back while the others threw flags and blew their whistles, struggling to untangle the mess of flailing arms and legs. The crowd, of course, went wild until the whole thing was sorted out. Finally the refs called a game timeout while they decided on penalties and ejections. Coach beckoned us over to the sidelines.

"What the hell was that? You ran the sweep?" he shouted at me. "Who in God's name told you to run the sweep? Have you totally lost your mind?"

I bowed my head and took his **reproaches** as I waited for the game to resume. Little did he know his **harangue** was falling on deaf ears. Little did he know his go-to guy was basically playing for the other side.

*   *   *   *   *

---

dynamic: energetic
cursory: hasty
insatiably: ravenously

bellicose: combative
melee: brawl

reproaches: criticisms
harangue: rant

Halftime offered no **respite**. The negativity in the locker room was **pervasive**, and Coach went off on us in his best imitation of a sports movie coach—so over the top it could almost be considered a **parody** if he wasn't so legitimately upset. His face was red, his veins throbbed, and he spat more than once as he ripped us all to shreds.

I sat near the side of the room, slumped, as Dick applied an **emollient** to my cut. I kept waiting for Coach to **ascribe** all the blame to me, but he had words for everyone. Apparently my sorry play was making everyone look bad.

"Offensive line? Your play out there is **putrid**!" he shouted, more spittle showering from his lips. "No quarterback of mine is getting sacked four times in one half. Especially not against this team! Their defense isn't even all that **adroit**, and you're making them look like some **divine** line sent down from God above!"

I looked over at my **disheartened** teammates, and my guilt flared anew. They should all be blaming me. I should have been the **anathema** in this room, no one else.

"It's like watching assault and **battery** out there!" he shouted, pacing back and forth. "You're better than this, guys! We all know that you're better than this!"

Guys shifted in their seats, looked at the floor, hung their heads. This was supposed to be the most triumphant moment of our high school careers, and it was nothing but a huge disappointment. Thanks to me. Why had I hidden those cards? Why had I ever agreed to play that game in the first place?

How could I sit here and let these guys who had backed me up time and time again take a beating for my mistakes? *Because Gray and those guys are going to kill you otherwise*, a little voice in my head reminded me. I saw vividly the tree branch swinging toward my knees and clenched my jaw in determination. *There's no other way to* **appease** *them. They made that abundantly clear.*

---

respite: rest
pervasive: inescapable
parody: spoof
emollient: cream

ascribe: attribute
putrid: rotten
adroit: skilled
divine: almighty

disheartened: discouraged
anathema: disgrace
battery: abuse
appease: please

God, I just wanted this to be over. All I needed was a little more **forbearance** and it would be. I just had to get through this lecture and one more half of crap football, and I could go home and never look back.

Except that I would. With regret. Every single day of my life.

"And Riley!" Coach shouted.

My heart squeezed painfully. "Yeah, Coach?"

He put his hands on his hips and walked toward me. "I don't know how to make this any more **pellucid**. You do not call the plays out there, you got me? I call the plays," he said.

I swallowed hard. "Yes, Coach."

I had called plays before, and he never had a problem with it. Of course, nine times out of ten, those plays had been successful.

"I thought my game plan was fairly **trenchant**, but apparently I was wrong. Otherwise you wouldn't be all over the place out there," he said **condescendingly**. "Now, do I have to **delineate** the points for you again?"

"No, Coach," I said, my face burning. It had been a long time since I had been so **avidly denounced** by anyone, let alone the guy who had taken me under his wing. For the first time in a long time, Coach Rinaldi's belief in me was **equivocal**. I had never thought that could happen.

"Good. Now, if I see you get **lackadaisical** out there again, so help me God I'm gonna rip you a new one," he snapped. "You keep your head up. You scramble. And you hold on to the G.D. ball! You look like a freakin' amateur out there!"

I sunk a bit lower in my seat. It wasn't as if I could challenge the **veracity** of any of these criticisms.

He took a deep breath and stood up straight, surveying the team. "Now, men, that field out there is our **sovereign** territory. Am I right?"

---

forbearance: patience
pellucid: clear
trenchant: clear-cut
condescendingly: haughtily

delineate: lay out
avidly: enthusiastically
denounced: condemned
equivocal: doubtful

lackadaisical: careless
veracity: truth
sovereign: official

"Yeah!" Everyone shouted, relieved that the browbeating portion of the meeting was over and we were on to the pep talk part.

"So are we going to let these Dorchester losers come in here and crap all over our territory?" he shouted.

"No!"

"When you're **dispatched** from here, you're going to go out there and make me proud! Am I right?"

"Yeah!"

As my teammates riled themselves up, jumping out of their seats and cheering, it was all I could do to keep from throwing up right there on my cleats. They had no idea that this game was only going to get worse. That I was about to lead them straight into the gutter.

I only wished there was something—anything—I could do.

*   *   *   *   *

As I trudged back toward the field with the rest of the team, the marching band was out there doing its thing, playing the school's classic fight song. They may as well have been playing a funeral **dirge**, as far as I was concerned. All around me the guys were jumping up and down, getting primed, knocking helmets and slapping backs. All I wanted to do was run. We passed through the gates and onto the track that ran around the field, jogging by some bystanders who had lined up along the fence. A **medley** of voices shouted either insults or good wishes at me, but mostly insults. That was when I heard someone calling my name.

"Mike! Yo, Riley!"

At first I ignored it. I figured it was just one more vocal fan wanting to convey his **umbrage** with my first-half performance.

"Mike, man! We need to talk to you!"

That was when I recognized the voice as Ian's. I paused and found his face in the crowd. He was with Winter, who was waving

---

dispatched: sent   **medley:** assortment   **umbrage:** displeasure
dirge: death march

me over maniacally. Ian himself looked half-desperate, half-excited. I felt an unfounded surge of hope and jogged over to them to hear what they had to say. A couple of the guys on the team looked at me like I was insane, but I was getting used to that today.

"Dude, you have to stop this idiocy," Ian said under his breath. "Enough is enough."

I looked around, my face hot with humiliation and fear. Apparently Ian knew what was going on. I glanced at Winter and understood everything in one look. She had told him. She had told him about my plan. Part of me knew I should be angry at her betrayal, but I didn't have it in me. All my emotional capacity had already been used up.

"I'm sorry," Winter said. "I didn't know what else to do, so I called Ian. And I'm glad I did."

"You have to go back out there and save this game," Ian said.

"I can't," I whispered through my teeth. "Those guys are going to kill me if I don't win them their money back."

"No! You don't understand," Winter said. "We got them to **rescind** the deal."

I felt as if the earth had just tilted beneath me. If the deal was off, then weren't they going to kick my ass anyway? I glanced at my teammates, who were gathering on the sidelines. Any minute now they were going to start wondering where I was.

"What do you mean?" I demanded. "What did you guys do?"

"I went over there this morning, and we had a little talk with Gray," Ian said. "I tried to call you a zillion times before the game, you know. You really should answer your phone. Could have saved yourself a lot of trouble."

"Riley! You suck!" someone shouted, to the delight of the crowd.

"And **defamatory** comments," Winter added, rolling her eyes.

"I wasn't exactly in the mood to chat," I replied impatiently. "Now tell me what's going on."

---

rescind: take back   **defamatory:** slanderous

"Basically, Ian used his powers of persuasion to talk my brother and his friends out of betting on the game," Winter said quickly. "They were **phlegmatic** at first, but then—"

"I appealed to their pride," Ian said, looking mighty proud himself. "The last thing those guys want is for the Hillside football program to fall into **disrepute**. They didn't mind the idea of people **disparaging** *you* all over the place, but the alma mater was a different story."

"He made some **pithy** arguments, I gotta say," Winter told me, looking at Ian with admiration. "It's not easy to get my **pugnacious** brother to back down."

"But I did," Ian said. "When it comes down to it, those guys are still Hillside Cardinals at heart. They want to see Dorchester win this game about as much as you do."

I couldn't believe Ian's **largess**, walking into the lion's den like that to save my butt. He was a better friend than I had ever realized.

"Wait, so you're telling me I'm off the hook here?" I said, hardly daring to accept it. Who knew Gray was capable of granting such complete **clemency**? "I don't have to pay those guys back?"

Ian and Winter exchanged a look. "Well . . . not exactly," Ian said.

"Riley! What the hell are you doing over there?" Coach shouted, earning me some jeers from the immediate crowd. "Get with the team already!"

"Just one second, Coach!" I shouted back, my heart pounding. He looked at me like I was the most **enigmatic** being on earth before throwing up his hands and turning back to the guys.

"What do you mean, 'not exactly'?" I asked.

"Well, you're still going to have to **atone** for what you did," Ian said quickly. "It wasn't like they were going to eat all their losses, so we had to make a deal."

"What deal?" I could barely breathe.

---

phlegmatic: uninterested
disrepute: shame
disparaging: insulting

pithy: convincing
pugnacious: combative
largesse: benevolence

clemency: forgiveness
enigmatic: mysterious
atone: make up for

"We set up one last poker game. You against them," Winter said. "Winner takes all."

She had to be kidding. *Another* poker game. I thought neither of them wanted me to play anymore. Had everyone lost their minds?

"They loved it," Ian said. "Those guys are all about competition. Well, that and cold, hard cash."

I felt like I was going to be sick. "Me against the four of them? Are you guys insane?!" I said—rather **callously**, considering how **beneficent** they had been on my behalf. "That only gives me a one in five chance of winning. What if I lose? I don't have the money to pay them double! I'll be in an even bigger hole than I am now. How the hell is another poker game going to **ameliorate** my situation?"

"Well, for starters it means you can go out there and win this freakin' game," Ian said sarcastically. "I do believe I saw the scouts up in the box before, looking at one another like they were wondering why the hell they made the trip. Or are you no longer **aspiring** to play football in college?"

Okay. That hit home. Apparently Ian *could* be rather pithy.

"He's right, Mike," Winter said, laying her tiny hands on my shoulder pads. "Don't think about the poker game now. One thing at a time. And right now you have to play the game of your life."

I glanced at the field, where the marching band was just starting to make its way off. Any second the refs were going to get out on the field to start the second half. After everything I had done in the first two quarters, a comeback seemed next to impossible. I suddenly felt emotionally exhausted and **torpid**, like it would take every ounce of energy in me just to walk over to the bench and sit down. All day I had been counting on this thing with Gray being over by the end of the game, and now it wouldn't be. Even though there were benefits to this scenario, the thought of dealing with him and his friends later was overwhelming.

"We're down by two touchdowns," I said quietly.

---

callously: coldly   **ameliorate:** improve   **torpid:** lazy
beneficent: kind   **aspiring:** striving

"What's with all the **pessimism**? Two touchdowns is nothing!" Winter said. "You're Mr. Football Star, remember?" she added with a laugh. "Didn't you score like four touchdowns against the best defense in the league?"

Wow. Apparently Winter had become a bit of a fan on my behalf. But it didn't change the fact that I was a traitor—that I was the scum of the earth—and that I had done it all, it seemed, for no reason. If I had just picked up the damn phone before the game I would have known all of this and we would be winning right now.

"I don't know if I can do it," I told her.

"Well, I do," Winter said firmly. "*I* know you can. I believe in you, Mike. You can do anything."

"Aw! So **poignant**," Ian joked.

I automatically reached out and shoved him, and we all laughed. But when I looked back into Winter's eyes, I **surmised** that she really believed what she was saying. She really thought I could get out there and turn this sinking ship around. Then she glanced at Ian quickly, stood on her toes, and whispered in my ear.

"I kind of love you, you know?" she said.

My heart spasmed, and I felt a rush of pure elation. "Really?"

"Really," she said.

When she pulled back, she was smiling and her gorgeous green eyes shone. Somehow, the fact that she had **evinced** her feelings for me just then was all I needed. Suddenly I could feel my blood flowing again, my adrenaline pumping. I reached into all my **reservoirs** of strength and determination and energy and pulled myself up straight. After all the crap and misery I had endured over the past few weeks, Winter telling me she loved me was about the most incredible thing she could have done.

I looked around at my teammates, who were eyeing me with impatience, and at the crowd, which was getting psyched up. I felt better than I had in days. Winter was right. I could deal with Gray

| pessimism: negativity | surmised: figured out | reservoirs: reserves |
| poignant: moving | evinced: revealed | |

later. All that mattered now was winning this game. It was **incumbent** upon me to fix the mess I had made in the first half, to lead this team to a victory. And maybe, in the process, I would even solidify my future.

"Riley! Get your ass over here!" Coach Rinaldi screamed.

"Excuse me, guys," I said to my friends with a smile. "I have a game to win."

incumbent: essential

As I approached the first huddle at the **onset** of the second half, some **heckler** from the Dorchester stands shouted out a fairly lewd comment about my "mama," and hundreds of people laughed. I clenched my jaw, and my hands curled into fists. Little did this guy know the pain I was about to unleash on his team. In the next two quarters—one if I had my way—he and all his friends were going to watch Dorchester's lead **evaporate**. It was time for me to earn back a little bit of **dignity** here.

"All right guys! Huddle up!" I shouted.

We came together on the fifteen yard line, and I looked around at the faces of my teammates and friends. Their energy and desperation were palpable. All they needed was for me to be the leader I had always been for them, but I could tell that just then, some of them doubted that I could still do that. I swallowed hard, knowing that nothing could **negate** what I had done in the first half. But at the very least, I could try to make it up to them.

"Listen up, you guys, I know the first half sucked . . . well *I* sucked. I made **innumerable** mistakes, but I'm putting that all behind me now, and you guys need to do the same," I said firmly. "These guys are not that **formidable**. We can take them."

My confidence was **contagious**. I felt the adrenaline starting to course through the air as they murmured their assent.

"Now, clearly their left side is their weak link," I said. "Let's **exploit** that in this half. We're gonna work on those guys until they crack, and we're going to **eradicate** their lead. You with me?"

"Yeah!" they all cheered through their teeth.

---

onset: start
heckler: person yelling insults
evaporate: disappear

dignity: respectability
negate: cancel
innumerable: countless
formidable: challenging

contagious: spreading
exploit: use
eradicate: destroy

"Okay, I say we get out there and take it right to them," I said. "Let's go for the end zone right now, on the first play."

A few of the guys clearly loved this idea, but Daryl's brows came together beneath his helmet.

"Is that the play Coach called?" he asked.

Valid question, considering I had been warned, quite sternly, not to **counteract** Coach's orders. Everyone looked at me quizzically, and I knew that it was time to take charge of this team again. I had to be **intransigent** in my beliefs and in my game play, or they weren't going to trust me. If my team couldn't trust me, their quarterback, that would be our ultimate downfall.

"No, it's not," I said flatly. "But out here, I'm in charge, right?"

"Right!" they all chorused.

"Right," Daryl said again, nodding.

"Good. We're going with four wide receivers. D, you're my number-one man, but if you can't get open, I'm going with you, Kyle," I said. "Curtis, I need you on Trung, too. Double-team that bastard, okay?"

"You got it, Mikey," Curtis said.

"Good. You guys hold the line, and I'll put it in the end zone," I said. "Now let's do this."

The ref blew the whistle, and we broke from the huddle. I was about to change the course of this game from one that would go down in **infamy** to one that the Hillside fans would take pride in forever. My confidence and determination were **intemperate**. I was going to **demean** these Dorchester suckers, the way I had allowed them to do to me in the first half. Maybe even worse.

"What are you doing? Riley! What the hell are you doing?!" Coach screamed, **mystified** by our four–wide-out formation. He had, after all, called a conservative run play. Meanwhile, the Dorchester defense was scrambling, trying to figure out how to cover a formation they had never seen from us before.

"Cover that guy! Cover him!" I heard one of the linemen shout.

---

counteract: go against	**infamy:** shame	**demean:** degrade
intransigent: unyielding	**intemperate:** brutal	**mystified:** confused

I grinned. This was going to be too easy.

"Hike!" I shouted.

Everyone ran. The linemen clashed and our front four **demolished** their guys, giving me plenty of time.

"Riley! Riley! Throw the damn ball!" Coach shouted in desperation.

Not yet, coach, I thought, hearing nothing but my own breath, the grunts of the offensive line, my heart pounding in my ears.

Daryl was covered deep by the cornerback. The guy was all over him. My gaze shifted left, and I saw Kyle shake his defender with a sick stutter step. The guy hit the dirt and Kyle raised his arm. I pulled back, held my breath, and let the ball fly. There was a collective gasp in the stands as the ball soared through the air. Time stood still. Everyone turned to watch, and just like that the ball landed perfectly in Kyle's outstretched arms, right on the twenty-yard line.

Our stands exploded with uninhibited **merriment**.

"Go!" I shouted. "Go!"

Kyle took off, firing on all engines for the end zone.

"He's at the ten! The five! The one! Touchdown, Cardinals!" the announcer cried into his microphone.

I thrust my arms into the air in **ecstasy** as the screams of the **reveling** crowd surrounded me. Touchdown on the first play from scrimmage. That would show these guys who they were dealing with. I glanced at the clock as the team ran back to crowd me. Only fifteen seconds had ticked off, and we had cut their lead in half. Fairly **efficient** play, if you asked me.

I saw Kyle running toward me and I hugged him, lifting him off the ground. The crowd went berserk.

"We're gonna crush these guys!" I shouted.

"Yeah, baby!" Kyle shouted back.

And with that we jogged off the field toward our coach who, for all his lectures about obeying his orders, was grinning like he'd just won the Super Bowl.

---

demolished: destroyed
merriment: happiness

ecstasy: joy
reveling: celebrating

efficient: effective

* * * * *

After the game, which had turned into a total rout in the second half, I sat in Coach Rinaldi's office, listening to the distant celebrations of the Hillside fans. I was all showered and clean, dressed in my street clothes, and the band was still out there playing while the fans chanted. The final score was 45 to 23. We had scored six touchdowns in the second half. Dorchester had scored only one and missed the extra point. It was kind of embarrassing, actually. For them, of course.

Outside the glass door to the office, Coach talked to the scout from Penn State. *Penn State. Here to see me.* I still couldn't wrap my brain around it. The guy was at least six foot five, three hundred pounds, and looked fairly imposing in his suit and tie. He kept nodding, and I could see that whatever he was saying was pleasing the coach. Rinaldi's eyes gleamed with excitement.

Finally the door opened and I jumped to my feet, remembering my manners. This could be one of the most important meetings of my life.

"Mike Riley, I'd like you to meet Richard Klint, the football scout from Penn State," Coach Rinaldi said.

"Hello, sir," I said **cordially**, extending my hand.

"Call me Richard," he replied, his voice booming. His hand was huge and calloused and his grip firm. "It's a pleasure to meet you, son. A real pleasure."

"Thank you, sir . . . uh . . . Richard," I said.

He laughed and slapped me on the back. "Let's have a seat."

We did, and he pulled his chair close to mine so we were facing each other. Coach sat in his desk chair on the edge of his seat. A cheer went up outside, and Richard sat up a bit straighter.

"**Fanfare**'s still going on out there. That's all for you, you know," he said. "You were the **consummate** hero out there today."

---

cordially: agreeably   fanfare: cheering   consummate: complete

"Well, thanks. But it was a team effort," I replied.

"Humble, too," he said with a grin. "Listen, Mike. I like the way you played out there today. I like it a lot. We all know that first half was not your best, but you showed real heart and **conviction** coming out there the way you did in the second. That takes some real strength of character to put something like that behind you and to **elevate** your play the way you did. I was impressed."

"Th . . . thank you," I said.

The **irony** of these compliments was not lost on me. I wouldn't have had to show any strength of character if I hadn't been totally character-free in the first half and cheated my teammates to save my own skin.

"And you were playing with a fresh injury. That shows some real **endurance**," he said.

I was blushing now and touched my arm. "That was just **incidental**," I said. "Nothing big."

"I like this kid, Rinaldi!" Richard and Coach both laughed as if they were in on some private joke together. I shifted in my seat, my pulse racing with excitement. It seemed as if this meeting was going rather well. Though whether I deserved it, I had no idea.

"Your **fundamentals** are strong, but you also have your own **distinctive** style," he continued. "Coach tells me that touchdown pass to lead off the third was all you?"

I glanced at Coach uncertainly and he nodded, prodding me to take the credit. I guess he really wasn't mad about that.

"Yeah, well, I thought it would be good to show them that we weren't just going to slink off the field," I said. "I wanted to show them what we were made of."

Richard's face lit up. "That's great, son. I like that attitude. You **exemplify** everything we look for in a leader at Penn State. I hope you haven't **predetermined** your college plans, have you?"

---

conviction: confidence
elevate: raise
irony: paradox
endurance: stamina

incidental: minor, unimportant
fundamentals: basics
distinctive: unique

exemplify: embody
predetermined: decided in advance

I was dumbfounded. *Yeah I have,* I thought. *I've wanted to go to your school my entire life. Just say the word and I'm there.* But somehow I managed to keep it together and not say too much. Didn't want to show him all my cards right up front.

"No, sir," I replied.

"Well, good. Because a decision like that takes a lot of **deliberation**, and you need to have all the facts," he said. "I'd love for you to come out and take a look at our program. In fact, don't just think of me as a football scout, think of me as an **emissary** for the entire school. We need a stand-up guy like you at our university."

A stand-up guy like me. Right. The guy who just spent thirty minutes of football taking a dive.

"Wow. That's great," I said. I had no idea what else to say.

"Great. I'll give your parents a call, and maybe we can meet up this weekend so I can extend the invitation to you all," he said. "I can't **disclose** the details of our offer until you come visit the school, but I can tell you there will be one. Although I expect after today you'll be **inundated** with offers. We scouts don't take a comeback like that lightly."

My entire mouth was dry. I felt as if I had done something **crafty**, eating dirt in the first half just so I could show what I was made of in the second. It was unbelievable how well this whole negative situation had turned out. Thank God Ian had gone all **meddler** on me and talked to Gray. Otherwise I'd be sitting out there with my head hanging between my knees, afraid to show my face.

"All right. I should go and give those other guys a crack at ya," Richard said, standing and extending his hand. "They're lining up to talk to you, but I trust you're gonna make the right decision. Am I right?" he asked with a wink.

I shook his hand and smiled. "Yes, sir."

"Richard!"

"Okay! Okay! Richard," I said.

---

deliberation: thought   **disclose:** reveal   **crafty:** sly
emissary: representative   **inundated:** flooded   **meddler:** one who interferes

"Talk to you soon, kid."

Coach ushered him outside, then stuck his head back in. "I'm going to say good-bye to him, then I'll bring in the guy from Michigan," he said. "You sit tight. You're gonna be here a while," he added with a grin.

"Okay," I said, still baffled.

He closed the door, and I sat back down in my chair and stared at the wall, unable to believe the way this day had turned around. A scout from Penn State was wooing me. He wanted me to come play for one of the **dominant** football teams in the country. Ever so slowly, my lips curled into a self-satisfied grin. For the first time in a while, I was **optimistic** about my future. For the first time in a while, I felt on top of the world.

*   *   *   *   *

By the time I was done meeting and greeting all the scouts, I was feeling quite **content** with myself. It seemed as if every last one of them was determined to talk me into coming to their school. Suddenly, my options were endless, and I couldn't wait to talk to my parents. They were going to be beside themselves.

My **jollity** was cut short, however, when I came around the corner in the hallway and found Gray, Lenny, and Rick waiting for me. Perfect. Just what I needed to **overshadow** an otherwise triumphant moment— **harassment** from this band of goons. At least Ogre was, for some reason, absent. I was **loath** to go anywhere near them, but they had already spotted me. There was no escape. I walked over, my head now hanging.

"What's up, fellas?" I said.

Gray and Rick wore their old red and black Hillside varsity jackets to show their support with the rest of the fans, while Lenny had

---

dominant: strongest   **jollity:** merriment   **harassment:** hassle
optimistic: hopeful   **overshadow:** darken   **loath:** reluctant
content: happy

gone with his usual black leather, apparently too cool to get with the program.

"Hey, Mike! Great game today!" Rick said in his usual chipper manner. "You really **persevered** out there. Those Dorchester idiots are still licking their wounds."

I blinked. Not the negative welcome I was expecting, but I would definitely take it. Gray, however, reached up and smacked Rick on the back of the head. Apparently there was some **discord** among the group about how I should be treated.

"Ow! What?" Rick said, touching his head and grimacing. "I'm just saying he played well."

"Wake up, Ricky. This is still the guy that cheated us out of our hard-earned cash," Lenny said gruffly.

"Exactly," Gray said, rounding his shoulders. He looked me up and down and sneered. "That was some **exemplary** play out there, though, Riley," he said sarcastically. "Did you have some good meetings with all those scouts?"

"Yeah," I said uncertainly. I raised my chin and looked him in the eye, hoping to win back some of my pride. "There's some interest."

"That's great, kid. You're still the golden boy," Gray said. "Too bad no one around here will ever know what a complete **fraud** you are."

He reached up and slapped his hand down on the back of my neck, hard. I resisted, but he managed to pull me toward him in his death grip. Fear squeezed my heart. Most of the fans had long since gone home, and there would be no one around to witness it if these guys ganged up on me. Maybe I could put up a good fight—after all, Rick was kind of a wuss—but there was no way I could overpower both Gray and Lenny.

"Come on, you guys," I said. "Winter and Ian said we had a deal."

"We do," Lenny told me, rubbing his hands together. "We just

---

persevered: endured   exemplary: outstanding   fraud: phony
discord: disagreement

want to make sure you know to take that deal seriously. After all, we wouldn't want to have to **propagate** some rumor about the Hillside hero fixing a game to right a gambling debt."

My heart swooped in my chest. "You wouldn't."

"Wouldn't we?" Gray said. "We could **debunk** your whole image just like that," he said, snapping the fingers of his free hand. "So don't mess with us, all right? You better show up at that poker game, and you better be ready to pay up."

"Okay," I said, as he tightened the vice on my neck. "Okay. I got it."

"Good," he said, shoving me away. I stood up, his fingerprints raw on my skin. "Otherwise you might not have the **longevity** to even make it to Michigan or USC. You get me?"

"Yeah," I said, nodding. Damn, this kid sure had the menacing thing down.

We all heard footsteps and looked up to see my parents entering through the gym lobby doors. The moment they spotted us, my mother's face creased with concern.

"Michael?" she said.

"That's our **cue**," Lenny announced.

Great. What could be better for the ego than to be saved by my mommy and daddy?

"Good game tonight, man. Really," Gray said **congenially**, patting me on the back. "We'll see you soon."

The three guys **sauntered** off together, passing my parents by on the way out the door. They even congratulated my mom and dad on my performance, and my parents looked relieved. They **erroneously** thought their *first* impression had been wrong when they believed these guys were threatening me. By the time I joined the two of them, they were both beaming with pride.

"Michael! What an incredible game!" my mother said, planting a kiss on my cheek.

"I met a couple of those scouts on their way out. Everyone wants

---

propagate: generate
debunk: disprove
longevity: endurance

cue: signal
congenially: pleasantly

sauntered: strolled
erroneously: in error

to come by the house tomorrow and meet you, son. Including the guys from Penn State," my father said.

"I know. I can't believe it," I said, forcing a smile.

My father patted me on the shoulder. "You did it, kiddo. You're gonna get that scholarship."

"I know. Thanks, Dad," I said.

Inside, my stomach was in knots. Lately, absolute comfort and happiness were proving to be **elusive** things. Whenever I was up, it wasn't for very long. There was always someone or something waiting around to remind me of the mess I had made.

"Everything okay, son?" my dad asked.

Apparently my acting skills weren't up to par. For a split second I thought about confessing everything. It was clear to me, in that moment, that coming clean was **inevitable**. Sooner or later they were going to call the bank, and even if all the money was miraculously back in place by that point, they would get a statement and see that it had once gone down to zero. I would have to explain why I had emptied my account. Eventually they were going to know what I had done.

But now was not the time. They were so excited for me just then, and I didn't want to take that away from them.

"Yeah! Totally!" I replied. "Just a little tired."

"Well, you'll have to get your second wind," my mother said. "We're going out to celebrate."

"Okay," I said with a smile. "Let's do it."

May as well enjoy what could be my last day as the perfect son.

---

elusive: evasive   inevitable: unpreventable

The big poker game was being held at Rick's family's **ostentatious** mansion on the outskirts of town. Gray was **adamant** from the beginning that he would be the one to pick the location. He didn't trust me as far as he could throw me, basically, so he didn't want it to be at my house or Ian's, and I guess he wanted to avoid his own house since I had already managed to cheat them there. So Rick's place it was.

Rick lived up the hill from Ian and was pretty much the only guy I knew who was even more **affluent** than my best friend. Back when he was in school, people always wondered why he didn't hang out with other kids in his own tax bracket, but I understood. Those people saw Rick as a dorky, scrawny, wannabe football player. He didn't belong with them. So Gray and his friends on the team took him under their wing. I had always thought that was cool of them— that their charity in Rick's case meant that they were, in fact, kind people. Lately I had started to question that theory.

I was both extremely nervous and hopeful as I approached the front door. After tonight I might be able to get this **onerous** burden of guilt off my back. Not to mention the even more onerous debt. Or, of course, I might end up dead at the bottom of a ditch some-where when Gray and his friends realized that, even if they won, I had no way to pay them back.

What the hell am I doing? I wondered, holding my breath. I felt like I was standing on the doorstep to hell. But still, for some rea-son, I reached out and rang the bell.

Rick came to the door a few moments later. He grinned when he saw me standing there.

---

ostentatious: showy   **affluent:** wealthy   **onerous:** troublesome
adamant: forceful

"Mike Riley! How you doing, man?" he asked.

It was amazing how, even after everything that had happened, Rick's attitude toward me hadn't changed at all. It was as if he was proud to welcome me into his house.

"Watch your step," he said as he led me into the **capacious** front hall. "My parents are in the middle of **refurbishing** the place, so there's a lot of crap everywhere. Sorry about that."

"Oh, no problem," I said, stepping over a drop cloth. A towering ladder was propped up against the two-story-high wall, and the chandelier above was covered with another cloth. Half the ornate wallpaper had been stripped down and the walls beneath were bare and dotted with spackle.

"We're playing in the dining room," he said, his voice echoing off the high walls as he led me through a door to the right. "They're already done in there, so it's a little less cluttered. Though I have to apologize for the décor. The **artisan** they hired got a little **zealous** with the Native American theme."

Like I cared even the slightest bit about the décor. I was worried for my life, here.

Rick pushed open a pair of heavy double doors, and together we stepped into the **opulent** dining room. He was certainly right about his parents going over the top. They had definitely not gone for an **austere** look. The sideboard and counters around the table were crammed with Native American **artifacts**, everything from headdresses and beads to a bow and arrow to what appeared to be a buffalo skull. The color **palette** was all browns, oranges, and reds, and the chandelier of the freshly **burnished** wooden table was decorated with feathers and dream-catchers. I could have stared at this stuff all day if it wasn't for the small crowd of people at the far end of the huge table. A crowd that included not only Gray, Ogre, and Lenny, but also Winter and Ian.

"What are you guys doing here?" I blurted.

---

capacious: roomy	**zealous:** impassioned	**artifacts:** relics
refurbishing: renovating	**opulent:** fancy	**palette:** range
artisan: craftsman	**austere:** simple	**burnished:** polished

They looked so serious that I briefly thought Lenny and Ogre had **abducted** them or something, to use them as collateral if I lost.

Okay, so I watch too many movies. But seeing them there was that unexpected.

"They came to play," Gray said as Rick and I joined them.

"What do you mean?" I asked Ian. "Are you gonna be my **surrogate** or something?" I asked with a nervous laugh. "Play in my place in case something happens to me?"

I glanced nervously at Ogre and Lenny, who were standing behind Gray like a couple of sentries, acting all **aloof**. Their expressions didn't change at all. Apparently they didn't think I was funny, which put me even more on edge.

"No. We're going to play *with* you," Winter said, glancing at her brother. "These guys have agreed to a game of three on three. Whichever team ends up with the most chips at the end of five hands, wins. Evens the playing ground a little bit, right, Gray?" she added pointedly.

Ogre and Lenny exchanged a look and Gray nodded resolutely. I could tell none of these guys were very happy about the new rules, but apparently Winter had somehow persuaded her brother into this fairer course of action. I couldn't believe she had stuck her neck out there on my behalf in this way. Apparently she really *did* love me. I could have kissed her right then and there if I didn't think her brother would instantly tear me to shreds.

"This way we won't be here all night," Gray said, cracking his knuckles. "We all have better things to do than watching you squirm."

"*I* don't," Lenny said, clenching his jaw. Clearly he really just wanted me to suffer.

"You guys don't have to do this," I told Ian and Winter, even though I felt buoyed by the way in which they had **cleaved** themselves to me. It felt so much better with them backing me up.

---

abducted: kidnapped   **aloof:** standoffish   **cleaved:** stuck
surrogate: substitute

Although I had no idea whether Winter could actually play. Of course, this didn't seem like the appropriate time to quiz her about that.

"All right. Just so we're all clear, here's the deal," Gray said, looking around at all of us. "Me, Ogre, and Lenny are playing Mike, Ian, and Winter in five hands."

"You're not playing?" I asked Rick.

He shrugged. "We figured I should sit out since it's my house."

I nodded. Yeah, right. More like he should sit out because he was their least effective player.

"Whichever team ends with the most chips, wins," Gray continued. "If you guys win, Mike's debt is wiped clean."

Lenny grumbled at this point, and Gray shot him a silencing glare.

"If we win, you guys not only owe us all the money we win tonight, but also all the money Mike won from us after he cheated the other night," Gray finished, saying the last few words through his teeth.

I felt sick to my stomach. That was so much money I could barely even fathom it. "Can I talk to my friends for a second?" I asked.

Gray nodded. "You have one minute."

I pulled Winter and Ian aside and lowered my voice. "Listen, I appreciate you guys being so **solicitous**, believe me, but where the hell are we going to get that kind of money?"

Ian looked me in the eye, his expression firm. "Don't worry about it," he said.

My heart dropped. "Dude, I can't let you put up all that cash. I can't **advocate** that."

"You don't have a choice, man," Ian said. "I'm doing it. If we lose—which we will not—I'll just have to cut back on my lifestyle a little bit."

---

solicitous: concerned   **advocate:** supporter

"Ian—"

"I hear a life of **privation** is good for the soul," Winter interrupted with a smile.

"Totally," Ian said, grinning as well. "Come on, man. We have no other choice. Let's just get this over with."

I was so grateful at that moment I could have hugged him, but I didn't. I knew Gray and the other guys would mock me for the rest of the night if I did, and I was going to be under enough strain as it was.

"You tools ready yet?" Gray asked.

"Thanks, buddy," I said to Ian. "I owe you big time."

"You better believe it," he said.

I took a deep breath and squared my shoulders. "All right," I said to Gray. "Let's do this."

Gray offered his hand and we shook, sealing the deal. There was no turning back now. After just five hands of poker, my fate would be sealed.

*   *   *   *   *

After two hands of play, our teams seemed to be fairly even. Gray had won the first pot, which was thankfully not that big. All of us had **constrained** our betting while we sized one another up. On the second hand, all my questions about Winter's poker abilities had been answered. She had won the pot, slightly larger than the first, after some **canny** betting. Ogre was so **confounded** that she beat him, he had actually grown **animated** for a second, demanding to see her cards. He had studied everything for a good five minutes before finally **conceding** that her flush was valid and that it did, in fact, beat his straight.

Now we were on our third hand. The room was deathly silent as Ian, Gray, and Lenny stared at one another, trying to discern who was for real and who was bluffing. They were the only three left in

---

privation: being deprived
constrained: restricted

canny: shrewd
confounded: confused

animated: overly lively
conceding: accepting

this hand. Even though it pained me to do so—considering we were only playing these games to save my ass—I had folded early on a seriously crappy hand, wanting to hold on to as many of my chips as possible. I had to be smart in this game, not prideful.

"I think you're bluffing," Gray said finally, watching Ian, who didn't even blink. "It's totally **speculative**, of course, but I think you're bluffing. So I see your bet, and I raise you double."

He tossed his chips into the pot where they clinked against the others. I quickly calculated the amount in the center of the table and saw dollar signs. Winning this hand would definitely help me. It would give our team a little breathing room, which we sorely needed.

Ian leaned forward and tossed his chips in, seeing Gray's bet without a word. I saw Gray's Adam's apple bob up and down. He wasn't expecting Ian to do that so casually.

Everyone looked at Lenny. After betting the farm in the first two hands, he was almost **bereft** of chips. He narrowed his eyes, bending his two **pliable** hole cards back and forth between his hands. Clearly he was nervous. It was like he had forgotten how to bluff.

"Screw it. I'm in," he said. And he shoved at least half his chips into the center of the table.

Gray sighed, irritated. I was practically salivating. If Lenny lost this hand they were going to be seriously down.

"Okay. Dealing the river," Rick said.

He flipped the card over and no one moved.

"I'm in," Gray said finally, tossing in a few more chips.

Ian followed suit, keeping his mouth shut. Lenny smirked and pushed the rest of his chips into the pot. Unbelievable. Lenny was going all-in. If he lost, he would be out of the game. Then it would be two against three in favor of us. Didn't he **apprehend** how tonight's game was working?

"All right. Let's see what everyone's got," Rick said.

---

speculative: theoretical   **pliable:** flexible   **apprehend:** perceive
bereft: without

"Four of a kind, baby!" Lenny cried, standing up and slapping his cards down with a triumphant grin. There they were, all four tens—two in the hole, two on the table.

Gray looked relieved. "That beats me," he said, slapping hands with Lenny as he stood as well. "What about you, O'Connor?"

I glanced warily at Winter, who looked extremely pale under the dim light of the chandelier. Ian kept his expression **stolid** as he turned over his hole cards. I glanced quickly from them to the center of the table, and my heart caught.

"Holy crap. He's got a straight flush," I said.

"Yes!" Winter cheered, jumping out of her seat and flinging her arms around Ian's neck.

Gray and Lenny's faces fell. "No way! No freakin' way!" Lenny shouted. He lunged at Ian, shouting **aspersions**, and Ian jumped out of his chair, backing himself and Winter up and out of harm's way. My heart hit my throat. Ogre shot out of his seat, grabbing Lenny's arm as Gray tried to control him as well. I got up and put myself between the guys and Ian, my pulse pounding through my veins. If anyone was going to be **assailed** here, it should be me.

"Dude! Calm down!" Gray said, his muscles flexing.

"He cheated! He freakin' cheated! I know he did. Check his pockets! Check the cards!" Lenny shouted, **repudiating** his loss. He strained against his friends, and I clenched my fists, ready for a fight. He didn't look like he was going to remain **tractable** for very long.

"He didn't cheat," Ogre said quietly. "He just beat you."

Lenny's eyes widened, and for a second I thought he was going to **buffet** his friend, but gradually the fight started to go out of him.

"Dude, just go upstairs and calm down," Gray said, releasing his grip on Lenny's shirt. "You're out of the game."

Lenny yanked himself away from his friends and pushed his hands over his greasy hair. For a second I thought he was going to

---

stolid: unemotional
aspersions: slanderous insults

assailed: attacked
repudiating: refusing to accept

tractable: controllable
buffet: strike

freak out again, but instead he cursed under his breath and stormed out of the room. No one moved. A minute later we heard a far-door slam.

Gray looked at Ian. "Take your chips, man," he said tersely.

Ian did, and then we all got back to the game.

*　　*　　*　　*　　*

On the fourth hand, Winter folded quickly. She seemed to have an **affinity** for holding on to her chips, which I was grateful for. Her winnings and holdings were going to make up a big chunk of our final pot. I, however, decided to stay in on this one. After the flop I had a pair of kings and a queen, and the rest of the flop cards were low, which meant that if the other guys had pairs, they were lower than mine. It was the first time the cards hadn't stuck me in an **adverse** situation. I saw Gray's bet and raised him double. Ogre stayed in and Ian folded.

"Dealing the turn," Rick said.

I held my breath, hoping against hope for another queen. I didn't get it. The turn was a four. But still a low card. A pair of kings was still a decent hand, and I couldn't give up now. Not on my first good hand of the night. Then Gray helped me out a bit. He folded—with obvious **reluctance**.

"Your bet," Rick said, glancing at me.

I placed a few chips in the pot—enough to make Ogre realize how confident I was. Maybe a bold move would **repulse** him and he would fold. But Ogre was **restive** and wouldn't do what I wanted. Without flinching, he saw my bet.

All righty then. So much for my plan. Rick started to deal the river, but Ogre cut him off.

"Wait. Raise," he said, ever **concise**. Then he tossed *triple* his bet into the pot.

---

affinity: preference　　**reluctance:** hesitance　　**restive:** resistant to control
adverse: unfavorable　　**repulse:** drive away　　**concise:** exact

My heart dropped. Winter and Ian both squirmed. Okay. This was a **conundrum**. What cards could Ogre possibly have? Was he just bluffing? It was impossible to tell. The guy never changed facial expression even when he *wasn't* playing poker.

But come on. All I needed was a king or a queen on the river and I would have either two high pair or a high three of a kind. He couldn't beat that, right? Whatever. I couldn't back down now. I had to make a leap of faith.

"I'll see that," I said, tossing the chips in.

I heard Winter intake a sharp breath and ignored her. I was fine. Of course the butterflies in my stomach lacked my total **credulity**. I tried to keep them at bay, breathing slowly in and out.

You're fine, I told myself. *It's going to be fine.*

But I only had a few chips left. And if Ogre took this pot . . .

"Dealing the river," Rick said.

He flipped the card over. It was a six.

Okay. That's good. You still have a pair of kings, I told myself. *He's got nothing.*

Ogre placed his final bet.

"I call," I said, equaling his chips.

Come on, I thought. *I need this. I need this one . . .*

"Let's see," Ogre grunted, lifting his chin ever so slightly at me.

"Pair of kings," I said, forcing a confident smile to my face.

Everyone stared at Ogre.

Please let me win this . . . please let me win this . . . please let me—

And for the first time all night, Ogre smiled.

Oh, crap.

"Seven-high straight," he said, turning his cards over.

And there it was. A straight. Right in front of my eyes. Somehow I had allowed myself to grow **complacent**, and I had entirely missed the components right there on the table. Ian groaned. Winter sunk

---

conundrum: problem   **credulity:** willingness to believe   **complacent:** unconcerned

in her seat. Gray and Ogre high-fived as bile rose up in my throat. I had just lost half my team's chips on a stupid, idiotic play.

*   *   *   *   *

After four hands of play, we **aggregated** our chips and compared the totals with Gray so we would all know where we stood for the fifth and final hand. Winter, Ian, and I were down. Not by much, but we were down. One of us had to win the fifth hand, or my life, basically, was over. Rick dealt the hole cards, and all the muscles in my shoulders coiled. I was afraid to look at them. This was it. The **culmination** of all the misery and tension and guilt and fear. It all came down to this one hand.

I took a deep breath, closed my eyes, and said a quick prayer. Then I checked my cards. An eight and a six, suited. Not horrible, but not the greatest draw in the world either.

Next to me, Winter shifted in her seat. Not a good sign. I glanced at Ian, and when he looked at me I knew he didn't have the cards. Apparently, I was staying in no matter what. One of us had to pony up and play, or it would be over right here and now.

"Gray?" Rick said.

"I'm in," Gray replied, tossing a couple of chips in the pot.

Ogre grunted and followed suit.

Ian sighed and shook his head. "Can't do it, man," he said, tossing his cards toward Rick. "I fold."

"Tell me you have good cards," Winter whispered to me. I **subjugated** my fear and remained expressionless. I knew Gray and Ogre were watching me closely. Winter sighed. "I fold."

"And then there was one," Gray said with an amused smirk.

I wanted to jump over the table and deck him. The compulsion was so great that I even came out of my seat a little bit. But Winter laid her hand on my arm, and I stayed in my chair. I had to maintain

---

aggregated: collected   **culmination:** climax   **subjugated:** subdued

some kind of **propriety**. If I attacked Gray, I knew the deal would be off. Besides, if this hand went south for me, we were all going to be brawling soon enough. Why rush it?

"Mike? Your bet," Rick said.

I stared Gray in the eye, picked up a couple of chips, and saw his bet. In a different situation I might have even raised him, but I was playing for my life here and needed to be a little bit **stingy**. But still, I was going to **avenge** my last loss. I was going to put this guy in his place. He and that cocky smile of his were going down.

I hoped.

"Dealing the flop," Rick said.

He turned the three cards over. There were two eights and a ten.

Yes! Yes, yes, yes! I thought. Rick had given me a three of a kind. A great start. It took every ounce of willpower I had to keep from smiling.

I looked at Gray. He blew out a sigh and raised the bet. His cards weren't great. I could tell. That sigh **belied** his confidence. He was only raising to try to throw me off. I wanted to look at Ian to see if he confirmed my suspicions, but I couldn't look at anyone for fear of giving something away.

Ogre saw Gray's bet, and I called. I didn't want to throw more money in there than I needed to. At least not yet.

"Dealing the turn," Rick said.

His hands were shaking as he turned the card over. The tension was even getting to him. I couldn't believe it when I saw the card. The six of hearts. I had a full house, and the river hadn't even been dealt yet.

Everyone looked at Gray. "I'll raise," he said, throwing in a few chips. My heart skipped a couple thousand beats. What the hell did he have in his hand? He put his elbow on the table and placed his fist to his mouth. These were all such obvious tells. Was it all an

---

propriety: appropriate behavior

stingy: cheap

avenge: take vengeance for

belied: contradicted

act? If it was and I fell for it, I would be **vituperating** myself for the rest of my life.

But my gut told me he was bluffing. I had to go with my gut. I knew I had been wrong in the past, but this was too important. I had to trust myself.

Ogre folded with a grunt and stared down at the table. Ian sighed and leaned forward, placing both hands over his face. One down, one to go. It was down to me and Gray.

I stared Gray in the eye. "I raise," I said, throwing double the chips into the pot.

"Oh my God," Winter said under her breath.

My stomach turned with doubt. *What am I doing? What am I doing?*

But I just kept staring at Gray. *Give up,* I willed him. *Give up now.*

"Fine," he said. "I call."

His chips clicked against the others. The pot had grown big enough that if I won the hand, I would get out of here scot-free.

"Okay. Dealing the river," Rick said.

He slapped the card down. Another six. Gray didn't move. He didn't even blink. He just stared at the cards as if he could see through them. The six didn't improve my hand, but did it improve his? Well, clearly. Because even if he had nothing before, he had a pair of sixes now. Not enough to beat me though.

"I check," Gray said.

"I call," I replied, my throat dry.

For a moment, no one moved. This was it. The moment that would decide the rest of my life.

Whatever happens, just be a man, I told myself. *Take it like a man.*

"Let's see both hands," Rick said.

Gray turned his cards over. A ten and a jack. "Two pair," he said.

Quaking, I turned my own cards over. "Full house."

"Yes!" Ian shouted, standing up so fast his chair fell over.

---

vituperating: condemning

Winter squealed and threw herself into my arms as I stood. I hugged her tightly, reveling in the most **sublime** moment of my life. It was over. It was really and truly over.

"What happened?" Lenny demanded, running back into the room for the first time in an hour. Clearly he had been hovering outside, listening for our reactions. "What happened?"

"They won," Gray said flatly. He looked disgusted. Clearly, losing was **unpalatable** to him. Not that I could blame him. No one liked to lose. Especially after being cheated. But we had made a deal, and he had come up with the terms. He had to accept the loss.

"What? No way! When I left, you guys had a **tenable** lead!" Lenny shouted, growing red.

"Dude, calm down," Gray told him. "They won and it was fair. We made a deal. It's over." Talk about taking it like a man.

"Yeah, it is!" Ian shouted, reaching out to slap my hand.

"No. No way," Lenny said. "I'm not losing out on all that cash after he cheated. One more game, Gray," he said. "I'll go up against him one-on-one."

Gray put his hand on Lenny's shoulder and looked him in the eye. "When I say it's over, it's over," he said. "It doesn't matter what happened in the last game. *This* game, we lost. You're not going to **coerce** me into changing my mind."

Lenny stared me down for a long moment, and his severe **aversion** to me was clear. I had a feeling that if he ever saw me on the street, we would be in for the throw-down of our lives. But for now, he was going to back down. Because Gray was the man in charge. And I wasn't important enough to merit a **coup**.

Gray walked around the table, and as he approached, Winter reached out and clutched my hand, as if she was afraid Gray might try something. Instead, he offered his own hand in congratulations.

"Nice game, man," he said.

"Thanks."

sublime: glorious	**tenable:** able to be held	**aversion:** dislike
unpalatable: distasteful	**coerce:** force	**coup:** takeover

He gripped my palm and pulled me toward him. My heart swooped, but I looked him in the eye.

"You better never come near me again if you want to live, got me?" Gray said.

I swallowed hard. "Got it."

Gray released me and turned toward the door. "Let's get out of here. I need a beer."

Ogre got up and loped off after Gray. Lenny also reluctantly followed. Rick, after looking at us uncertainly, finally scurried off as well. Apparently doing as Gray said was more important than leaving random people alone in his own house.

"Well. Guess we'll be hanging out at your house from now on," Winter said dryly.

I laughed and leaned down to give her a nice, long kiss. Then I looked at Ian, and we both grinned. I was free. And I owed it all to them.

Chapter Fourteen

I sat in the basement of our local VFW hall, looking around at the **legion** of gambling addicts who had gathered for that evening's Gamblers Anonymous meeting. I had finally, *finally*, **liberated** myself by confessing everything to my parents, and they had been, understandably, mystified. They had **queried** me for hours, growing more and more frustrated and hysterical as I related the details of what I had done. My guilt and **remorse** had been almost **overpowering**, but I had managed to sit there and take it all—their anger, their disappointment, their **scorn**—everything. When the shock had finally died down, they had insisted that I join GA, and I had been going to meetings for four weeks now. At this point, it was my home away from home.

At first I had dreaded coming to the meetings. I had this **perception** that the place was going to be filled with gruff, overweight losers—older guys who had nothing better to do with their time than to **squander** their cash. And there were some guys like that, but the more meetings I attended, the more I realized that there was no way to **generalize** the people that came to these things. The people here were old and young, male and female, white, African American, Asian American. The only **attribute** we all had in common was that we had a problem and had finally come to admit it.

Every meeting was the same. People filed in and took their seats in an **orderly** fashion, then one of the more entrenched members got up to run the meeting. Each week there was a speaker, someone who got up to tell the story of how he or she had hit rock bottom. They were stories of **reckless** betting and reprehensible behavior. Stories that inevitably ended up with the speaker finding him- or

---

legion: multitude
liberated: freed
queried: questioned
remorse: regret

overpowering: overwhelming
scorn: disdain
perception: understanding
squander: waste

generalize: make assumptions
attribute: characteristic
orderly: tidy
reckless: irresponsible

herself a **solitary outcast**, shunned by family and friends. Some of these people had been in jail, had rendered their families penniless, had been on the verge of suicide. Listening to them was **therapeutic**, but also scary. I recognized myself in the beginnings of their stories—the inability to stop betting, the lust for the thrill of a win—and realized I could have ended up in a much worse place than I had.

I was so grateful that I had my parents and my friends.

After the meetings, the vibe became more **sociable** as everyone gathered to chat, sip coffee, and eat the snacks that some of the members provided. I had met some cool people, including a couple of guys and a girl who had graduated from my high school within the past five years. The more people like that I met, the more I realized I wasn't alone and the more comfortable I became.

Tonight it was finally going to be my turn to share my story. I was a little **reluctant** to do so. I had a feeling that some of the more hardened guys in the group were going to think my story was lame compared to some of the things they had gone through. But I had to do it. It was all part of the process.

"And now I believe that one of our newer members would like to take the floor," Betty Cross, one of the older ladies, said into the microphone. "Come on up, son," she said, gesturing to me.

I stood up and walked to the microphone, looking out at the group. Even though I had felt **nurtured** by many of the members, I expected some people to look away or **scoff** at the pretty boy in his varsity jacket. But when I looked out at their faces, the **predominant** expression was one of interest and concern. I could do this. These people were just like me. They wanted to help.

"Hi," I said into the microphone. "My name is Mike, and I have a gambling problem."

"Hi, Mike!" they chorused back at me.

And somehow just **promulgating** the issue made me feel better. I took a deep breath and began to tell my story.

solitary: alone	**sociable:** friendly	**scoff:** express scorn
outcast: pariah	**reluctant:** hesitant	**predominant:** prevailing
therapeutic: medicinal	**nurtured:** cared for	**promulgating:** proclaiming

*   *   *   *   *

"An A, baby! Did I mention that I got an A?!" I cried, pulling my history paper out of my bag and holding it up. Ian glanced at me from behind the wheel of his car and rolled his eyes. "Oh . . . and what's this?" I said, yanking out my English midterm. "Oh, yeah! Another A!"

"Dude, if you don't quit shoving your grades down my throat, I'm going to drive this car into a tree," Ian said.

But he smiled. He knew how important it was that I had done well on my midterms. It was a **momentous** day. I had aced everything and was back on the honor roll, the team was on its way to the state finals in football, and Winter and I were doing well. I was finally starting to feel like myself again.

The only black cloud hanging over me was my parents. I knew that they were still disappointed in me, and I was going to have to earn back their trust, but these grades would go a long way to help me in that **pursuit**. I had been working my butt off for weeks, and it was finally paying off.

Ian pulled his car up at the end of my driveway. "Okay. We're here. Get out," he said flatly.

"Cheer up, man," I said. "Bs and Cs aren't *that* bad."

Ian punched me hard on the shoulder and I laughed and got out of the car. As he drove off, I made a beeline right for the mailbox. Once upon a time I would check the mail only **periodically**—when I knew the new *Sports Illustrated* was coming or if I had ordered something off the Internet. Now I checked it every single day. I was waiting for the most important letter of my life.

I held my breath and popped open the little plastic door. There, under all the junk mail and bills, was a fat, white envelope. For a second I thought it was a **mirage**, but after I shook my head and blinked, it was still there. I reached in and yanked it out, showering the other envelopes all over the cold ground.

---

momentous: important   **periodically:** occasionally   **mirage:** illusion
pursuit: job

There it was—the blue and white Penn State logo in the top left corner. My name and address right in the center. I quickly ripped the package open and pulled out the letter.

> Dear Mr. Riley,
> Congratulations! We are pleased to inform you of your acceptance to Pennsylvania State University and the guarantee of your full athletic scholarship!

There it was. Words in black and white **proclaiming** that my dream had come true. Even after everything. After all the mistakes I had made, all the things I had done that could have **sullied** my reputation and killed my chances for good, all the **obstacles** I had placed in my own way, I had achieved my ultimate goal. I had **subsisted**. And I had been accepted to one of the most **prominent** football programs in the country, not to mention one of the best schools. I knew I was going to be nothing but a **tyro** on that team full of all-stars and future NFL players, but I couldn't wait to learn from them. I couldn't wait to experience everything that was coming my way.

I could barely **repress** the shout of joy that was bubbling up in my throat. Penn State's head coach had called me himself last week to let me know that this was coming—as he did with all his top recruits—but having this **tangible** proof in my hands was beyond anything I had ever felt before. I was going to **retain** this letter for the rest of my life. It was my ticket out of Hillside, my ticket to a new life of success and **prosperity**.

"I did it," I said to myself, giddy. "I got in!"

I grabbed up all the stuff from the ground and ran into the house to call my parents. I couldn't **recall** ever having felt so overjoyed and relieved and vindicated in my entire life. It was time to celebrate.

---

proclaiming: announcing
sullied: tarnished
obstacles: barriers
subsisted: persisted

prominent: well-known
tyro: beginner
repress: hold back
tangible: real

retain: keep
prosperity: economic well-being
recall: remember

*   *   *   *   *

The following night I was behind the counter at the Hillside Burger King during an extreme **lull**, staring at the purple Formica wall across from me. Okay, so my life of success and prosperity was going to have to wait a little while. Right now I still had a debt to pay back. Right now I was still a minimum-wage grunt.

This job was another part of my deal with my parents. Aside from the required GA meetings, they had agreed to let me take a part-time job even though football season was still on. In fact, they had insisted on it. I would use any meager **remuneration** I received to start paying back the money I had taken out of my bank account, and I would work here until it was all paid back or until college started, whichever came first. Suffice it to say, I was taking as many extra shifts as possible to **truncate** my sentence.

The door opened, and in walked Ian and Winter. I stood up a little straighter and smiled. Thank God. Someone to talk to other than Boris, my **corpulent** manager, and Carlos, the skittish fifteen-year-old who compared everything that happened in his life to another scene out of *Star Wars*.

"Yo, burger boy. Get me a Whopper with cheese and a chocolate milkshake," Ian said loudly, slapping his hand down on the counter.

"Ha ha," I said, leaning over to give Winter a quick kiss.

"Do I look like I'm kidding?" Ian asked.

"Sorry," Winter said. "I tried to talk him out of coming, but he wanted to see you in your uniform."

"That's okay. I can **tolerate** him as long as he brought you," I said, giving her another kiss.

"Where's my burger, beyotch?" Ian asked.

I **squelched** the urge to smack him upside the head and instead put his order in. "I need a Whopper with cheese," I said into the microphone. Behind me in the kitchen, Carlos got to work putting

---

lull: slow period
remuneration: pay

truncate: shorten
corpulent: fat

tolerate: endure
squelched: stifled

the burger together. I grabbed a cup and placed it under the shake machine's spout. The **mechanism** whirred to life with a groan as if it hadn't been used in decades.

"What are you doing here anyway, man?" I asked Ian as I handed over his shake. "It's Friday."

"Oh, yeah! The Friday night game," Winter said, wide-eyed. "What gives?"

"Yeah, well, I **suspended** that crap," Ian said. He took a long pull on his straw and placed the cup down on the counter. "A couple of the guys came by the house tonight, but I **rebuffed** them. They were a little **miffed**, but I think it's time to move on, don't you?"

"Why's that?" I asked.

"Well, call me **paranoid**, but I don't really want to be responsible for the downfall of any more of my friends," he said. "I mean, look at you, man. That hat alone is a **travesty**."

I stood up straight. "Come on," I said, spreading my arms wide and executing a little turn. "You don't like my look?"

Ian shuddered comically, and I smirked.

"Actually, I'm a big **proponent** of the hat," Winter stated. "I love a man in uniform."

"Yeah, you do," I said, leaning toward her again.

"Okay. You guys are gonna make me barf up this shake before I even get to the burger," Ian said.

"Well, I'm sorry, man. I didn't mean for you to have to cancel the whole game," I told him. "If it's me you're worried about, don't be. I don't plan to **relapse** any time soon."

"Or ever," Winter said firmly.

"That's what I meant," I replied, blushing.

"It's not just about you, man. I mean, Texas Hold 'Em was a **novelty**, but it's over. I sense the **imminent demise** of that particular trend," Ian said.

"Do you?" I asked with a smirk.

---

mechanism: machinery	**paranoid:** suspiciously fearful	**relapse:** backslide
suspended: stopped temporarily	**travesty:** joke, mockery	**novelty:** something new
rebuffed: snubbed	**proponent:** advocate	**imminent:** nearly at hand
miffed: annoyed		**demise:** death

"Yeah. It's **proliferated** to the point where it's not cool anymore," Ian said.

"And we all know you have to be on the cutting edge of cool," I said, playing along.

"Exactly," Ian said, leaning his elbows on the counter.

"So what's next?" Winter asked. "You going to open a strip club or something?"

Ian raised his eyebrows as if considering this idea. "Nah. Too messy. Too many permits involved," he said. "I'm gonna do something much more **radical**."

"Oh yeah? What's that?" I asked.

"I've decided to put my **latent** math abilities to use for good instead of evil," Ian said. He stood up and squared his shoulders, prepping for a serious announcement. "Kids, I'm joining the math team."

Winter and I looked at each other, stunned into silence for exactly one second before we cracked up laughing.

"What?" Ian cried. "I think I can still **salvage** their season! Come on, Mike! What? You're the only one who can be a joiner?"

And just like that, Ian—who had saved me so many times before—saved me once again. This time from an evening of complete Burger King boredom.

---

proliferated: increased rapidly, multiplied

radical: extreme
latent: dormant

salvage: save

A

abase: *v* undermine (13).

abate: *v* stop (15).

abdicating: *n* giving up (57).

abducted: *v* kidnapped (143).

aberration: *n* atypical event (11).

abetting: *v* encouraging (95).

abhor: *v* hate (14).

abide: *v* tolerate (120).

abject: *adj* spiritless (54).

abnegation: *n* giving up (63).

abort: *v* end abruptly (58).

abrasive: *adj* irritating (21).

abridged: *adj* shortened (106).

abruptly: *adv* suddenly (109).

abscond: *v* leave secretly (47).

absolution: *n* forgiveness (48).

abstain: *v* not partake (53).

abstruse: *adj* difficult (63).

abysmal: *adj* absolutely wretched (64).

accede: *v* give consent (62).

accelerating: *v* speeding up (84).

accentuated: *v* accented (85).

accentuating: *v* accenting (19).

accessible: *adj* within reach (98).

acclaim: *n* applause (62).

accolades: *n* positive acknowledgments (62).

accommodating: *adj* considerate (102).

accomplice: *n* assistant (esp. in wrongdoing) (21).

according: *v* giving (86).

accosted: *v* attacked (60).

accusatory: *adj* blaming (113).

acerbically: *adv* bitterly (16).

acquiesced: *v* gave in (14).

acquired: *v* taken (27).

acrimony: *n* hatred (26).

acumen: *n* intelligence (16).

acute: *adj* sharp (60).

adamant: *adj* forceful (141).

adept: *adj* skillful (26).

adhere: *v* stick (105).

adjacent: *adj* nearby (18).

admonished: *v* scolded (64).

adorned: *v* decorated (96).

adroit: *adj* skilled (18, 122).

adulation: *n* praise (86).

advantageous: *adj* favorable (89).

adversary: *n* enemy (25).

adverse: *adj* unfavorable (148).

adversity: *n* hardship (85).

advocate: *n* supporter (144).

affable: *adj* gracious (101).

affectation: *n* pose (110).

affinity: *n* preference (148).

affluent: *adj* wealthy (141).

aggregated: *v* collected (150).

aggrieved: *adj* wronged (106).

agile: *adj* nimble (84).

agitated: *adj* nervous (31).

agnostic: *adj* unsure of the existence of God (103).

alacrity: *n* eagerness (29).

alias: *n* fake name (104).

allay: *v* ease (15).

allegation: *n* accusation (110).

alleviated: *v* eased (29).

allocated: *v* set aside (106).

alluded: *v* hinted (52).

aloof: *adj* standoffish (143).

altercation: *n* quarrel (106).

ambiguous: *adj* vague (117).

ambivalent: *adj* undecided, conflicted (115).

ameliorate: *v* improve (127).

amenable: *adj* agreeable (72).

amenities: *n* conveniences (97).

amicable: *adj* friendly (111).

amplified: *adj* boosted (86).

anathema: *n* disgrace (122).

anecdote: *n* brief story (102).

anguish: *n* pain (16).

animated: *adj* overly lively (145).

anomaly: *n* irregularity (120).

antagonist: *n* enemy (83).

antecedent: *n* predecessor (102).

antidote: *n* cure (91).

antipathy: *n* dislike (93).

antiquated: *adj* old (17).

antiseptic: *adj* extremely clean (98).

antithesis: *n* opposite (7).

anxiety: *n* worry (95).

apathetic: *adj* spiritless (7).

appallingly: *adv* shockingly (11).

apparently: *adv* seemingly (14).

appease: *v* please (122).

appraise: *v* judge (89).
apprehend: *v* perceive (146).
arboreal: *adj* treelike (96).
archetypal: *adj* exemplary (6).
ardor: *n* zeal (6).
arid: *adj* dry (84).
artifacts: *n* relics (142).
artisan: *n* craftsman (142).
ascertain: *v* figure out (104).
ascribe: *v* attribute (122).
aspersions: *n* slanderous insults (147).
aspiring: *v* striving (127).
assailed: *v* attacked (147).
assess: *v* evaluate (5).
assiduousness: *n* diligence (117).
assuaged: *v* eased (103).
assurances: *n* promises (114).
asylum: *n* mental institution (116).
atmosphere: *n* mood (83).
atone: *v* make up for (126).
attaining: *n* achieving (112).
attribute: *n* characteristic (155).
atypical: *adj* unusual (23).
audacious: *adj* bold (1).
audible: *adj* able to be heard (96).
augmenting: *v* adding to (91).
auspicious: *adj* lucky (25).
austere: *adj* simple (142).
avarice: *n* greed (52).
avenge: *v* take vengeance for (151).
aversion: *n* dislike (55, 153).
avidly: *adv* enthusiastically (123).
awe: *n* amazement (94).

B

balked: *v* stopped short (49).
banality: *n* ordinary nature (115).
bane: *n* burden (90).
banishing: *v* exiling (22).
banned: *v* barred (84).
battery: *n* abuse (122).
bedecked: *adj* dressed (83).
begrudge: *v* disapprove (4).
behemoth: *n* something huge (105).
belated: *adj* late (106).
belied: *v* contradicted (151).
bellicose: *adj* combative (121).
belligerent: *adj* hostile (53).
benefactor: *n* donor (54).
beneficent: *adj* kind (127).
benevolent: *adj* kind (110).
benign: *adj* harmless (90).

bequeathed: *v* endowed (54).
berated: *v* criticized, chewed out (91).
berating: *n* criticizing, chewing out (15).
bereft: *adj* deprived, without (46, 146).
betray: *v* prove unfaithful to (116).
bewildered: *adj* confused (89).
biased: *adj* prejudiced (9).
bilked: *v* cheated (29).
blemish: *v* taint (48).
boast: *v* brag (89).
boisterously: *adv* loudly, rowdily (8).
bombastic: *adj* overblown (1).
boon: *n* blessing (6).
braggart: *n* boaster (85).
brandished: *v* held as a weapon (111).
brazen: *adj* defiant (4).
breach: *n* violation (4).
brusquely: *adv* bluntly (49).
brutality: *n* savagery (85).
buffer: *n* cushion (85).
buffet: *v* strike (147).
burnished: *adj* polished (142).
buttresses: *v* supports (109).
bypass: *v* avoid (87).

C

cacophony: *n* harsh noise (60).
cadence: *n* rhythm (58).
calamity: *n* disaster (64).
calculating: *adj* scheming (66).
callously: *adv* coldly (127).
camaraderie: *n* brotherhood (51).
candor: *n* honesty (49).
canny: *adj* shrewd (145).
cantankerous: *adj* cranky (116).
capacious: *adj* roomy (142).
capitulate: *v* give in (50).
carousing: *v* frolicking (90).
castigating: *v* punishing (60).
catalog: *n* list (103).
catalyze: *v* inspire (58).
catastrophic: *adj* disastrous (18).
caustic: *adj* scathing (51).
cavorting: *v* frolicking (45).
censuring: *v* scolding (115).
challenge: *v* disagree with (111).
chapped: *adj* rough (84).
charitable: *adj* for charity (2).
check: *n* restraint (74).
cherished: *v* appreciated (59).
circuitous: *adj* roundabout (85).
circumlocution: *n* talking in circles (113).

circumspect: *adj* cautious (56).

clairvoyant: *adj* possessing of a sixth sense (51).

clamor: *n* noise (4).

clarity: *n* clearness (116).

cleaved: *v* stuck (143).

clemency: *n* forgiveness (126).

coerce: *v* force (153).

cognizant: *adj* aware (45).

coherent: *adj* sensible (111).

collusion: *n* secret agreement (114).

colossal: *adj* huge (61).

combative: *adj* warlike (58).

commensurate: *adj* equal (95).

commiserating: *v* sympathizing (91).

commodious: *adj* spacious (48).

comparable: *adj* equivalent (86).

compassion: *n* pity (29).

compassionate: *adj* sympathetic (115).

compensate: *v* pay (93).

complacent: *adj* unconcerned (149).

complemented: *v* matched (83).

composed: *adj* calm (87).

compounded: *adj* combined into one (96).

comprehend: *v* understand (117).

comprehensive: *adj* extensive (63).

compulsion: *n* need (90).

compunction: *n* guilt (48).

conceding: *v* accepting (145).

conceivable: *adj* imaginable (86).

conciliatory: *adj* appeasing (111).

concise: *adj* exact (148).

concisely: *adv* sharply (114).

concocting: *v* creating (64).

concordant: *adj* agreeing (116).

condemnation: *n* blame (91).

condescend: *v* talk down (73).

condescendingly: *adv* haughtily (123).

condolences: *n* sympathies (50).

condone: *v* excuse (61).

conduct: *n* normal behavior (4).

confidant: *n* one to tell secrets to (48).

configuration: *n* setup (85).

conflict: *n* battle (84).

confounded: *adj* confused (145).

congealing: *adj* becoming solid (49).

congenially: *adv* pleasantly (139).

consensus: *n* agreement (87).

conserve: *v* save (89).

consolation: *n* comfort (91).

conspicuously: *adv* distinctly (72).

constrained: *v* restricted (145).

consummate: *adj* complete (134).

contagious: *adj* spreading (131).

contemplated: *v* thought about (57).

content: *adj* happy (137).

contentious: *adj* argumentative (106).

contrite: *adj* sorry (114).

conundrum: *n* problem (149).

convergence: *n* gathering (117).

convey: *v* pass on (111).

conviction: *n* confidence (135).

cordially: *adv* agreeably (134).

corpulent: *adj* fat (159).

corrective: *adj* counteracting (64).

corroboration: *n* corroboration (13).

corrosive: *adj* damaging (115).

counteract: *v* go against (132).

coup: *n* takeover (153).

crafty: *adj* sly (136).

credulity: *n* willingness to believe (149).

crescendo: *n* climax (35).

crude: *adj* unrefined (11).

cuckold: *v* cheat on (13).

cue: *n* signal (139).

culmination: *n* climax (150).

culpable: *adj* guilty (30).

cumulative: *adj* total (91).

cunning: *adj* crafty (26).

cursory: *adj* hasty (121).

curtail: *v* shorten (117).

D

daunting: *adj* intimidating (109).

deadpanned: *v* said matter-of-factly (36).

dearth: *n* shortage (37).

debacle: *n* catastrophe (18).

debase: *v* demean (28).

debilitating: *adj* weakening (118).

debtor: *n* one who owes money (93).

debunk: *v* disprove (139).

deceive: *v* mislead (42).

decibel: *n* loudness (34).

decisive: *adj* conclusive (117).

decisively: *adv* with certainty (17).

defamatory: *adj* slanderous (125).

deferential: *adj* respectful (120).

deferment: *n* temporary delay (115).

defiantly: *adv* boldly (30).

deficit: *n* shortage (7).

deft: *adj* skillful (7).

degradation: *n* humiliation (112).

deleterious: *adj* harmful (57).

deliberately: *adv* purposefully (120).

deliberation: *n* thought (136).
delineate: *v* lay out (123).
demean: *v* degrade (132).
demeanor: *n* outward manner (24, 92).
demise: *n* death (160).
demolish: *v* destroy (34).
demolished: *v* destroyed (133).
demonize: *v* portray as evil (30).
denigrate: *v* belittle (52).
denounced: *v* condemned (123).
deride: *v* ridicule (24).
derivative: *adj* copied (71).
desecrating: *v* profaning (120).
desiccated: *adj* dried up (80).
designs: *n* schemes (30).
desolate: *adj* barren (62).
despondency: *n* hopelessness (54).
destitution: *n* poverty (93).
deter: *v* discourage (52).
detractors: *n* naysayers (88).
deviant: *adj* twisted (70).
devious: *adj* cunning (114).
devoured: *v* ate greedily (4).
dignity: *n* respectability (131).
digression: *n* deviation (43).
diligent: *adj* dedicated (56).
diminutive: *adj* small (52).
dirge: *n* death march (124).
disavow: *v* refuse to acknowledge (61).
discern: *v* detect (7).
disclose: *v* reveal (42, 136).
discombobulated: *adj* confused (67).
discomfited: *adj* embarrassed and perplexed (62).
disconcerted: *adj* confused (65).
disconcerting: *adj* upsetting (62).
discord: *n* disagreement (138).
discrepancy: *n* disagreement (42).
disenfranchised: *adj* excluded (10).
disgruntled: *adj* discontented (10).
disheartened: *adj* discouraged (38, 122).
disheveled: *adj* in disarray (61).
disingenuous: *adj* insincere (14).
disparaging: *v* insulting (126).
disparate: *adj* different (10).
dispatched: *v* sent (124).
disregarded: *v* ignored (118).
disrepute: *n* shame (126).
dissembling: *v* being deceptive (14).
dissipated: *v* scattered (76).
dissuade: *v* advise against (35).
distinctive: *adj* unique (135).

distracted: *adj* diverted (109).
divert: *v* redirect (111).
divine: *adj* almighty (122).
divisive: *adj* dividing (38).
divulged: *v* revealed (115).
dominant: *adj* strongest (137).
dour: *adj* harsh (47).
douse: *v* soak (90).
drab: *adj* cheerless (116).
drub: *v* trounce (62).
dubiously: *adv* doubtfully (16).
duplicates: *n* copies (110).
duplicitous: *adj* sneaky (13).
duress: *n* threat (55).
dynamic: *adj* energetic (121).

E

earnest: *adj* serious (62).
ebbed: *v* eased (111).
ebullient: *adj* enthusiastic (45).
eclectic: *adj* varied (84).
ecstasy: *n* joy (133).
ecstatic: *adj* overjoyed (86).
effaced: *v* erased (38).
efficacious: *adj* effective (120).
efficient: *adj* effective (133).
effrontery: *n* disrespect (58).
effulgent: *adj* shining (83).
egregious: *adj* flagrant (37).
elaborate: *adj* extravagant (14).
elated: *adj* happy (9).
elevate: *v* raise (135).
elicited: *v* drawn forth (40).
elucidated: *v* made clear (48).
elude: *v* evade (57).
elusive: *adj* evasive (140).
embellished: *v* enhanced (45).
embezzle: *v* swindle (110).
embittered: *adj* bitter (112).
emissary: *n* representative (136).
emollient: *n* cream (122).
emote: *v* express emotion (74).
empathize: *v* feel compassion for (16).
emphatically: *adv* with emphasis (116).
empirical: *adj* based on experience (37).
enamored: *adj* fond (93).
encroach: *v* trespass (118).
endorse: *v* support (114).
endurance: *n* stamina (135).
engender: *v* produce (51).
enhance: *v* increase (114).
enigmatic: *adj* mysterious (126).

enmity: *n* hostility (16).
ennui: *n* boredom (35).
entailed: *v* involved (56).
entangled: *v* trapped (115).
enthralled: *adj* captivated (70).
ephemeral: *adj* short-lived (45).
epitome: *n* ideal example (5).
equanimity: *n* composure (52).
equitable: *adj* fair (27, 113).
equivocal: *adj* doubtful (123).
eradicate: *v* destroy (131).
erroneously: *adv* in error (139).
erudite: *adj* learned (10).
eschewing: *adj* avoiding (10).
espousing: *v* supporting (94).
essential: *adj* necessary (115).
euphoria: *n* great happiness (8).
evaluate: *v* assess (117).
evanescent: *adj* fleeting (76).
evaporate: *v* disappear (131).
evinced: *v* revealed (128).
exacerbate: *v* add to (66).
exaggerate: *v* overstate (113).
exalting: *v* applauding (86).
exasperated: *v* irritated (4).
exculpate: *v* clear from guilt (110).
excursion: *n* trip (10).
execrable: *adj* detestable (57).
executed: *v* carried out (84).
exemplary: *adj* outstanding (138).
exemplify: *v* embody (135).
exhort: *v* urge strongly (38).
exigent: *adj* demanding action (54).
exonerate: *v* clear (80).
exorbitant: *adj* excessive (73).
expedient: *adj* worthwhile (20).
expedite: *v* speed up (117).
expeditiously: *adv* promptly (23).
expiate: *v* make amends for (59).
exploit: *v* use (131).
expunge: *v* destroy (84).
extenuating: *adj* mitigating (114).
extolling: *v* raving about (71).
extraneous: *adj* excess (34).
extreme: *adj* severe (18).
extricating: *v* freeing (64).
extroverted: *adj* outgoing (23).
exult: *v* rejoice (27).

F

fabrication: *n* lie (89).
façade: *n* false appearance (22).

facile: *adj* effortless (18).
fanfare: *n* cheering (134).
fashioned: *v* made (96).
fastidious: *adj* picky (47).
fathom: *v* understand (13).
fatuous: *adj* foolish (39).
feigned: *v* faked (1).
feral: *adj* wild (85).
fervency: *n* enthusiasm (43).
fettered: *v* restrained (87).
fidelity: *n* faithfulness (16).
finite: *adj* having an end (24).
firebrand: *n* troublemaker (114).
flabbergasted: *adj* shocked (25).
flaccid: *adj* limp (60).
flagrant: *adj* obvious (41).
flanking: *v* bordering (109).
flee: *v* escape (110).
flippancy: *n* cheek, frivolity (113).
flouting: *v* defying (13).
foiled: *v* thwarted (1).
forbearance: *n* patience (123).
forlorn: *adj* sad (16).
formidable: *adj* challenging (131).
forsook: *v* abandoned (74).
fortitude: *n* strength (54).
foster: *v* encourage (17).
fraud: *n* phony (138).
fraught: *adj* full (50).
frenetic: *adj* frenzied (5).
frugal: *adj* thrifty (30).
fundamentals: *n* basics (135).
furtively: *adv* secretly (39).
futile: *adj* useless (110).

G

gargantuan: *adj* huge (109).
garish: *adj* gaudy (83).
garrulous: *adj* talkative (91).
generalize: *v* make assumptions (155).
genially: *adv* in a friendly manner (39).
glossy: *adj* sleek (24).
glutton: *n* ready recipient (27).
goading: *v* prodding (25).
graciously: *adv* politely (23).
gratuitous: *adj* unwarranted (15).
gravity: *n* seriousness (26).
grievous: *adj* grave (62).
grove: *n* area of trees (109).
grudgingly: *adv* reluctantly (9).
gruff: *adj* husky (109).
guile: *n* cunning (14).

H

hapless: *adj* unfortunate (36).
harangue: *n* rant (121).
harassment: *n* hassle (137).
hardy: *adj* robust (59).
haughty: *adj* arrogant (76).
heckler: *n* person yelling insults (131).
hegemony: *n* domination (34).
heinous: *adj* horrific(9).
hemorrhaging: *v* bleeding (80).
hiatus: *n* break (79).
hindrance: *n* obstacle (24).
hindsight: *n* retrospect (21).
hypocrisy: *n* deceitfulness (19).
hypothetically: *adv* theoretically (50).

I

ignominious: *adj* humiliating (54).
illicit: *adj* unlawful (39).
imitated: *v* mimicked (30).
immerse: *v* sink (86).
imminent: *adj* nearly at hand (160).
immoderate: *adj* excessive (118).
impassioned: *adj* excited (114).
impassive: *adj* expressionless (39).
impecunious: *adj* penniless (52).
imperative: *adj* necessary (16).
impertinent: *adj* rude (21).
impervious: *adj* impenetrable (14).
impetuous: *adj* impulsive (19).
impinge: *v* trespass (64).
implicit: *adj* implied (13).
impotent: *adj* useless (26).
impromptu: *adj* spontaneous (5).
impute: *v* attribute (119).
inane: *adj* silly (45).
incarnate: *adj* in the flesh (120).
incendiary: *adj* inflammatory (65).
incessantly: *adv* constantly (70).
incidental: *adj* minor, unimportant (135).
incinerate: *v* burn (39).
inclination: *n* desire (37).
inclined: *adv* predisposed (35).
incompetent: *adj* without skill (117).
inconsolable: *adj* beyond being comforted (41).
incontrovertible: *adj* indisputable (88).
increments: *n* increased amounts (36).
incriminating: *adj* proving guilt (110).
incumbent: *adj* essential (129).
indebted: *adj* owing gratitude (29).
indefatigable: *adj* untiring (75).
indescribable: *adj* beyond description (75).

indeterminate: *adj* unknown (118).
indigent: *adj* poor (80).
indignantly: *adv* angrily (72).
indolent: *adj* lazy (48).
indomitable: *adj* steadfast (83).
induce: *v* cause (57).
ineffable: *adj* beyond words (75).
ineffectual: *adj* worthless (76).
inept: *adj* unskilled (26).
ineptness: *n* incompetence (120).
inevitable: *adj* unpreventable (140).
inextricably: *adv* inescapably (73).
infamy: *n* shame (132).
infuse: *v* inject (24).
ingenious: *adj* clever (65).
ingenuous: *adj* honorable (61).
inhibit: *v* prevent (77).
inimical: *adj* antagonistic (75).
iniquity: *n* wickedness (61).
initiating: *n* starting off, setting up (33).
innate: *adj* inherent (2).
innocuous: *adj* harmless, trivial (113).
innumerable: *adj* countless (131).
inordinately: *adv* unusually (72).
insatiably: *adv* ravenously (121).
insinuating: *v* suggesting (72).
insipid: *adj* dull (30).
instantaneously: *adv* instantly (26).
instigate: *v* provoke (52).
insular: *adj* isolated (59).
integral: *adj* necessary (65).
intemperate: *adj* brutal (132).
interjected: *v* interrupted (65).
interminable: *adj* endless (55).
intimating: *v* implying (34).
intoned: *v* spoke musically (3).
intractable: *adj* unmanageable (66).
intransigent: *adj* unyielding (132).
intrepid: *adj* adventurous (56).
inundated: *v* flooded (136).
inured: *v* accustomed (76).
irascible: *adj* hot-tempered (52).
irony: *n* paradox (92, 135).
irrevocable: *adj* cannot be undone (94).

J

jollity: *n* merriment (137).
jubilation: *n* joy (8).
judicious: *adj* wise (50).
justified: *v* warranted (8).
juxtaposed: *adj* contrasted (89).

K

kinetic: *adj* related to motion or force (83).
knell: *n* announcing sound (40).
kudos: *n* praise (36).

L

laceration: *n* cut (119).
lackadaisical: *adj* careless (123).
laconic: *adj* mysteriously quiet (45).
languidly: *adv* lazily (45).
largess: *n* benevolence (126).
latent: *adj* dormant (161).
laudatory: *adj* praising (37, 87).
lavishing: *v* heaping on (48).
legerdemain: *n* sleight of hand (56).
legion: *n* multitude (155).
lenient: *adj* permissive (42).
lethargic: *adj* sluggish (42).
liability: *n* burden (80).
liberated: *v* freed (155).
licentious: *adj* immoral (61).
linchpin: *n* one that holds a group together (59).
lithe: *adj* gracefully athletic (120).
loath: *adj* reluctant (137).
longevity: *n* endurance (139).
lucid: *adj* clearheaded (42).
lull: *n* slow period (159).
lulled: *v* relaxed (58).
luminous: *adj* glowing (48).
lunacy: *n* madness (114).

M

maelstrom: *n* storm (39).
magnanimous: *adj* good-hearted (54).
maledictions: *n* curses (119).
malevolent: *adj* vicious (9).
malleable: *adj* easily influenced (101).
mandate: *n* order (80).
manifold: *adj* abundant (71).
maverick: *n* rebel (100).
mawkish: *adj* overly sentimental (101).
meager: *adj* weak (10).
mechanism: *n* machinery (160).
meddler: *n* one who interferes (136).
medley: *n* assortment (124).
melee: *n* brawl (121).
melodious: *adj* musical (8, 105).
mendacious: *adj* dishonest (1).
mercilessly: *adv* unrelentingly (41).
mercurial: *adj* unpredictable (52).
meritorious: *adj* worthy of honor (88).

merriment: *n* happiness (133).
metamorphosis: *n* transformation (105).
meticulous: *adj* careful (11).
miffed: *adj* annoyed (160).
mirage: *n* illusion (157).
mired: *v* stuck (16).
mitigated: *v* diminished (86).
mocking: *v* ridiculing (19).
moderate: *adj* mediocre (36).
modesty: *n* shyness (11).
modicum: *n* small portion (42).
mollified: *v* calmed (2).
momentous: *adj* important (157).
morass: *n* difficult situation (98).
morose: *adj* gloomy (41).
multifarious: *adj* intricate (83).
mundane: *adj* ordinary (33).
munificence: *n* generosity (3).
muttered: *v* murmured (100).
myriad: *n* great number (62).
mystified: *adj* confused (132).

N

nadir: *n* lowest point (41).
naïve: *adj* innocent (15).
nascent: *adj* new (69).
nefarious: *adj* wicked (49).
negate: *v* cancel (131).
negligent: *adj* neglectful (99).
neophyte: *n* beginner (10).
noisome: *adj* noxious (100).
nominal: *adj* insignificant (56).
nonchalantly: *adv* casually (26).
nondescript: *adj* indistinct (119).
notion: *n* idea (30).
notorious: *adj* unfavorably well-known (47).
novelty: *n* something new (160).
novices: *n* beginners (56).
noxious: *adj* poisonous (75).
nuance: *n* variation (103).
nurtured: *v* cared for (156).

O

obdurate: *adj* inflexible (38).
obfuscated: *v* confused (99).
oblivious: *adj* unaware (26).
obscure: *v* hide (76).
obsequiously: *adv* obediently (100).
obstacles: *n* barriers (158).
obstinate: *adj* stubborn (28).
obstreperous: *adj* noisy (56).
obtuse: *adj* dense (93).

odious: *adj* hateful (69).
ominous: *adj* foreboding (63).
onerous: *adj* troublesome (141).
onset: *n* start (131).
optimistic: *adj* hopeful (137).
opulent: *adj* fancy (142).
oration: *n* speech (57).
orderly: *adj* tidy (155).
ornate: *adj* excessively decorated (37).
oscillate: *v* waver (38).
ostentatious: *adj* showy (141).
ostracize: *v* banish (67).
outcast: *n* pariah (156).
ovation: *n* round of clapping (88).
overcome: *adj* overwhelmed (26).
overpowering: *adj* overwhelming (155).
overshadow: *v* darken (137).

P

pacific: *adj* peaceful (18).
palette: *n* range (142).
palliate: *v* ease (9).
pallid: *adj* pale (10).
palpable: *adj* noticeable, touchable (83).
palpitating: *v* throbbing (33).
panacea: *n* cure-all (105).
paradigm: *n* typical example (42).
paragon: *n* perfect example (87).
paramount: *adj* all-important (42).
paranoid: *adj* suspiciously fearful (160).
paraphernalia: *n* equipment (97).
pariah: *n* outcast (105).
parody: *n* spoof (122).
parsimony: *n* stinginess (2).
partisan: *n* follower (101).
patent: *adj* apparent (89).
pathetic: *adj* pitiful (27).
paucity: *n* shortage (27).
pejorative: *adj* negative (103).
pellucid: *adj* clear (123).
penchant: *n* fondness (93).
penitent: *adj* regretful (21).
penultimate: *adj* second-to-last (103).
penurious: *adj* stingy (49).
perception: *n* understanding (155).
perfidious: *adj* two-faced (81).
perfunctory: *adj* quick (64).
periodically: *adv* occasionally (157).
perks: *n* benefits (2).
permeated: *v* seeped through (40).
perplexed: *adj* baffled (34).
persevered: *v* endured (138).

perspicacity: *n* intelligence (77).
pertinacious: *adj* headstrong (74).
perused: *v* examined (18).
pervasive: *adj* inescapable (122).
pessimism: *n* negativity (128).
petulant: *adj* peeved (106).
philanthropic: *adj* humanitarian (93).
phlegmatic: *adj* uninterested (126).
pillaged: *v* looted (75).
pinnacle: *n* peak (107).
pithy: *adj* convincing (126).
pittance: *n* little bit (73).
placated: *v* appeased (38).
placid: *adj* calm (42).
platitudes: *n* dull remarks (101).
plaudits: *n* cheers (75).
plausible: *adj* believable (87).
plenitude: *n* abundance (76).
plethora: *n* abundance (56).
pliable: *adj* flexible (146).
poignant: *adj* moving (128).
polemic: *n* aggressive verbal attack (50).
portent: *n* omen (98).
pragmatic: *adj* sensible (66).
precipice: *n* cliff (61).
precluded: *v* prevented (10).
predetermined: *v* decided in advance (135).
predictable: *adj* unsurprising (4).
predilection: *n* preference (20).
predominant: *adj* prevailing (156).
premises: *n* property (84).
preponderance: *n* excessive number (34).
presage: *n* omen (55).
prescribe: *v* specify (35).
presumptuous: *adj* assuming (99).
pretense: *n* posturing (20).
pretentiously: *adv* pompously (29).
privation: *n* being deprived (145).
probity: *n* honor (74).
proclaiming: *v* announcing (158).
procrastinating: *v* delaying (17).
procure: *v* obtain (22).
prodding: *v* urging (15).
prodigy: *n* child genius (30).
profane: *adj* crude (21).
profusion: *n* excess (30).
prohibited: *adj* forbidden (22).
proliferated: *v* increased rapidly,
    multiplied (161).
prominent: *adj* well-known (158).
promulgating: *v* proclaiming (156).
propagate: *v* generate (139).

propensity: *n* preference (9).
propitious: *adj* promising (92).
proponent: *n* advocate (160).
propriety: *n* appropriate behavior (151).
prosaic: *adj* unimaginative (23).
prospects: *n* future opportunities (89).
prosperity: *n* economic well-being (158).
prowess: *n* great ability (35).
prudence: *n* good judgment (53).
prurient: *adj* lewd (70).
puerile: *adj* childish (13).
pugnacious: *adj* combative (126).
pulchritude: *n* beauty (69).
punctilious: *adj* strict (102).
pungent: *adj* strong smelling (34).
punitive: *adj* disciplinary (80).
pursuit: *n* job (157).
putrid: *adj* rotten (122).

Q

quagmire: *n* difficult position (40).
quaint: *adj* charmingly old-fashioned (95).
quandary: *n* predicament (92).
quell: *v* quiet, pacify (27, 94).
queried: *v* questioned (155).
querulously: *adv* grouchily (65).
quipped: *v* joked (28).
quixotic: *adj* bold (74).
quizzically: *adv* curiously (26).
quotidian: *adj* everyday (96).

R

radical: *adj* extreme (161).
railed: *v* protested (80).
rancorous: *adj* malevolent (26).
rank: *n* foul (34).
rapport: *n* personal connection (36).
rash: *adj* careless (74).
raucous: *adj* harsh (6).
razed: *v* flattened (75).
reap: *v* harvest (30).
rebuffed: *v* snubbed (160).
rebuke: *n* reprimand (46).
recalcitrant: *adj* disobedient (78).
recall: *v* remember (158).
reciprocate: *v* exchange in kind (72).
reckless: *adj* irresponsible (155).
reconcile: *v* settle (79).
rectitude: *n* righteousness (119).
redoubtable: *adj* formidable (57).
refracted: *v* reflected distortedly (98).
refurbishing: *n* renovating (142).

refute: *v* deny (22).
relapse: *v* backslide (160).
relegated: *v* demoted (64).
relished: *v* savored (27).
reluctance: *n* hesitance (148).
reluctant: *adj* hesitant (156).
remedial: *adj* special education (64).
remiss: *adj* irresponsible (17).
remorse: *n* regret (155).
remuneration: *n* pay (159).
renovated: *v* refurbished (95).
renowned: *adj* widely known (101).
repentance: *n* regret (70).
replete: *adj* full (37).
repose: *n* lie down (15).
reprehensible: *adj* unforgiveable, disgraceful (42, 113).
repress: *v* hold back (158).
reprieve: *n* delay of punishment (41).
reproaches: *n* criticisms (121).
reprobate: *adj* morally corrupt (103).
reprovingly: *adv* with scorn (63).
repudiating: *v* refusing to accept (147).
repulse: *v* drive away (148).
reputable: *adj* esteemed (95).
requisite: *adj* required (4).
rescind: *v* take back (125).
reservoirs: *n* reserves (128).
resilient: *adj* able to adapt (106).
resolutely: *adv* firmly (26).
resolved: *v* decided (15).
respite: *n* rest (122).
restitution: *n* payback (105).
restive: *adj* resistant to control (148).
retain: *v* keep (158).
retract: *v* take back (39).
revelers: *n* celebrators (83).
reveling: *adj* celebrating (133).
revered: *adj* honored (102).
rhapsodize: *v* speak emotionally (10).
ribald: *adj* offensive or course (59).
rife: *adj* overflowing (71).
roster: *n* list of players (2).
ruminating: *v* thinking (17).
ruse: *n* trick (41).

S

saccharine: *adj* overly sweet (96).
sacrosanct: *adj* sacred (101).
sagacious: *adj* wise (25).
sagely: *adv* wisely (24).
salivated: *v* drooled (83).

salutation: *n* greeting (65).
salvage: *v* save (161).
sanctioned: *adj* approved (3).
sanguine: *adj* confident (36).
sauntered: *v* strolled (139).
scathingly: *adv* cruelly (80).
scoff: *v* express scorn (156).
scorn: *n* disdain (155).
scouring: *v* searching (15).
scrupulous: *adj* careful (74).
scrutinizing: *v* examining (7).
scurried: *v* scampered (7).
semaphores: *n* signals (75).
seminal: *adj* unprecedented (33).
serendipity: *n* good luck (69).
serene: *adj* calm (71).
severe: *adj* extreme (16).
skeptically: *adv* doubtfully (22).
skirted: *v* went around (10).
slovenly: *adj* untidy (9).
sobriety: *n* soberness (17).
sociable: *adj* friendly (156).
solicitous: *adj* concerned (144).
solipsistic: *adj* self-centered (80).
solitary: *adj* alone (156).
solvent: *adj* financially sound (73).
somnolence: *n* sleepiness (61).
sophomoric: *adj* childish (36).
sovereign: *adj* official (123).
spacious: *adj* roomy (2).
speculative: *adj* theoretical (146).
spontaneously: *adv* impulsively (21).
sprite: *n* elf (96).
spurious: *adj* bogus (70).
squander: *v* waste (155).
squelched: *v* stifled (159).
stagnated: *v* gone stale (38).
staid: *adj* serious (103).
stellar: *adj* outstanding (83).
stern: *adj* serious (21).
stifle: *v* repress (21).
stingy: *adj* cheap (151).
stoic: *adj* unmoved (14).
stolid: *adj* unemotional (147).
strenuous: *adj* exhausting (119).
strident: *adj* loud (78).
stupefied: *adj* astonished (105).
subjugated: *v* subdued (150).
sublime: *adj* glorious (153).
subsisted: *v* persisted (158).
subterfuge: *n* deception, trickery (27, 98).
succinct: *adj* concise (14).

succumb: *v* give in (7).
sufficed: *v* been enough (84).
sullied: *v* tarnished (158).
superfluous: *adj* extra (105).
surfeit: *n* excess (76).
surmised: *v* figured out (128).
surreptitiously: *adv* stealthily (61).
surrogate: *n* substitute (143).
suspended: *v* stopped temporarily (160).

T

tacit: *adj* silently expressed (58).
taciturn: *adj* quiet (16).
tangential: *adj* peripheral (76).
tangible: *adj* real (158).
tantamount: *adj* equal (65).
tedious: *adj* tiresome (18).
temerity: *n* boldness (73).
temperance: *n* self-restraint (80).
tenable: *adj* able to be held (153).
tenuous: *adj* weak (81).
therapeutic: *adj* medicinal (156).
timorous: *adj* timid (72).
tirade: *n* rant (15).
tolerate: *v* endure (159).
tomes: *n* books (18).
torpid: *adj* lazy (127).
tractable: *adj* controllable (147).
tranquil: *adj* calm (41).
transgression: *n* violation (42).
travesty: *n* joke, mockery (160).
tremulously: *adv* shakily (13).
trenchant: *adj* clear-cut (123).
trepidation: *n* worry (22).
trite: *adj* unoriginal (15).
truculent: *adj* savage (36).
truncate: *v* shorten (159).
truncated: *v* shortened (64).
turpitude: *n* corruption (79).
tyro: *n* beginner (158).

U

umbrage: *n* displeasure (124).
uncanny: *adj* strange (20).
unconventional: *adj* different (21).
unctuous: *adj* oily (100).
undoubtedly: *adv* surely (95).
unencumbered: *adj* burden-free (85).
unpalatable: *adj* distasteful (153).
unrelenting: *adj* nonstop (58).
upbraided: *v* reprimanded (21).
usurp: *v* take over (120).

utilitarian: *adj* simple and useful (97).
utterance: *n* pronouncement (74).

V

vacillating: *v* wavering (104).
vacuous: *adj* unintelligent (70).
validate: *v* confirm (16).
vapid: *adj* dull (19).
vehemently: *adv* fiercely (13).
veneer: *n* façade (99).
venerate: *v* revere (42).
veracity: *n* truth (123).
verdant: *adj* green (35).
vestige: *n* sign (79).
vexed: *adj* annoyed (67).
vicariously: *adv* by proxy (102).
vicissitudes: *n* fluctuations (64).
vigilant: *adj* cautious, alert (107, 119).
vilifying: *n* slandering (15).
vindictive: *adj* spiteful (15).
vituperating: *v* condemning (152).
vivacious: *adj* lively (69).
vociferous: *adj* vocal (119).

W

wallowing: *v* indulging (15).
wan: *adj* sickly (59).
wane: *v* fade (18).
wanton: *adj* immoral (17).
wily: *adj* sly (39).
winsome: *adj* charming (19).
wistful: *adj* dreamy (64).
wrath: *n* anger (119).
wretched: *adj* extremely bad (62).
wry: *adj* ironically humorous (41).

Y

yoke: *n* burden (16).

Z

zealous: *adj* impassioned (142).

SPARKNOTES
Test Prep

Our study guides provide students with the tools they need to get the score they want...**Smarter, Better, *Faster.***

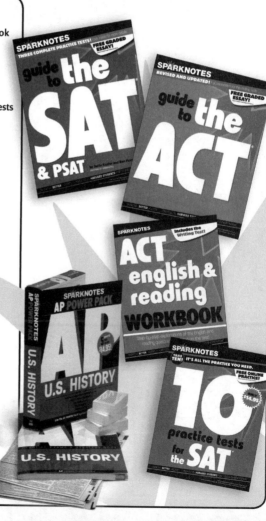